Death By Drowning

D1214972

Abigail Keam

# Death By Drowning
## A Josiah Reynolds Mystery

# Abigail Keam

**Worker Bee Press**

Abigail Keam

**Death By Drowning**
**Copyright © Abigail Keam 2011**

Library of Congress 2010919448

ISBN 978-0-615-42908-3

**Worker Bee Press**
PO Box 485
Nicholasville, KY 40340

For Diana,
Who shines like the Northern Star.

# By The Same Author

Death By A HoneyBee I
Death By Drowning II
Death By Bridle III
Death By Bourbon IV
Death By Lotto V
Death By Chocolate VI
Death By Haunting VII

## The Princess Maura Epic Fantasy Tales

Wall Of Doom I
Wall Of Peril II
Wall Of Glory III
Wall Of Conquest IV

# Death By Drowning

The author wishes to thank Stephen Powell, who consented to be a character, www.powellglass.com, Al's Bar, which consented to be used as a drinking hole for my poetry-writing cop, Kelly, and Morris Book Shop, www.morrisbookshop.com, which consented to be a meeting place for Meriah Caldwell and Josiah in the Josiah Reynolds series.

Also Anna Lowery and Susan Smith-Durisek for their comments.

Thanks to the Lexington Farmers' Market, which has given me a home for many years. www.lexingtonfarmersmarket.com

Special thanks to Neil Chethik for his unwavering support. www.neilchethik.com

And to my editor, Brian Throckmorton and Patti DeYoung

Art Work by Cricket Press www.cricket-press.com

Book Jacket by Peter Keam With much gratitude.

Abigail Keam

# PROLOGUE

He silently paddled the kayak through the chilly waters of the Kentucky River, alone except for occasional river otters slipping playfully down their muddy slides or the screech owl beckoning mournfully from a redbud tree ready to open its pink blossoms announcing spring in the Bluegrass.

There were no homes on this part of the river – just low sloping farmland on one side of the river and the high gray limestone wall of the Palisades on the other. He didn't need the lights of buildings to help navigate the river. He knew the curving green ribbon of water like his own flesh – besides, there was a full moon. He could see fine – just like the catamounts that roamed the Palisades. Every so often he could hear one of them scream. Their eerie cries might have given a lesser man pause, but his mind was made up.

Finally he came to one of the few sand beaches on the river and beached the beat-up, green kayak, dragging it upon the loose sand. On either side of the kayak were tied red gasoline cans. He cut the ropes binding them with quick, assured movements. He tugged on a waterproof bag, checked its contents of rags, matches and lighters, and then slung it across his back. He had several miles to trek before he reached his destination. He began the march. There was no doubt or wavering in his manner. His features showed no sign of the tension that was churning in his gut.

He was not going to waste any more time thinking of an alternative. He was determined. There was a vineyard to burn.

# 1

Death had stood on the doorstep and knocked on my door – but I didn't answer. I didn't die. There were days I wished I had – the pain was so great.

I don't remember very much except that I awoke once only to open one swollen eye slightly to see Matt, my best friend, reading to me. Over his shoulder stood Brannon, my late husband, observing the both of us. Seeing me conscious, Brannon said, "He's reading to you from the Book of Ruth."

Ruth, my favorite story from the Old Testament, told the tale of loyalty between two women facing starvation. When the mother-in-law, Naomi, tries to turn Ruth away in order to save her, Ruth says, "Where thou goest, I go; where you lodge, I lodge; your people shall be my people; your god shall be my god; where you die, there shall I also be buried."

It was too bad Brannon had never understood this concept of loyalty when alive. Now dead, he was nothing but a pile of dust in a cardboard box stored in my walk-in closet. *What was he doing here now?* Brannon turned so I could see my daughter asleep in a chair lodged in a corner. Loyalty. I smiled. At least, I think I smiled.

Matt turned a page and kept reading. I realized that I couldn't hear Matt. I thought to myself – *why can't I hear?*

"You're deaf, Josiah," Brannon said. "From the fall." He held out his hand. "Come with me."

*I'm not going anywhere with you. You abandoned me,* I thought in a huff.

"Where we're going, your anger won't matter. It will be forgotten."

*Go away, Brannon. Mad at you. Mad. Mad. Mad.*

"Ahh, Josey, you were always stubborn," he chided, his image fading.

Closing my good eye, I slipped back into a coma. I didn't awaken until several weeks later. I couldn't stand the intense pain and would have flung myself out a window – if I could have moved.

When my daughter begged the doctors to put me back into a medical coma, they refused. They were going to let me sweat it out. My daughter couldn't stand the screaming – my screaming.

I must be rotten deep inside the way I hated them, the very men and women who saved my life, but hate them I did. I loathed the way they thought they were doing me a great favor by prescribing measly dosages of pain medication. I reviled their condescension, their tired jokes and heartless procedures. That suffering is good for the soul is a fool's philosophy. I don't like pain and have no use for suffering.

Neither has my daughter.

I hazily remember bits and pieces of leaving the hospital – Matt leaning over me and holding my hand, mouthing goodbye; the doctors arguing with my daughter as she had the bandages, IV's, monitors and everything else, including me, packed up; the humming of the plane engines as I was flown to Key West where the medical profession doesn't frown on dispensing large dosages of painkillers.

I was later told the decision to move me to Key West was made on that day when I was shrieking like a lunatic about the unbearable throbbing on my left side . . . the side that impacted the cliff ledge . . . because the doctors wouldn't give me more morphine.

My daughter installed me in a three-bedroom bungalow complete with a pool on the ocean. She brought in her own physician's assistant to stay with me. Then what pain medication she couldn't get legally, she bought off the black market. I didn't scream again.

During the few times I was somewhat lucid, I tried to ask her what had happened, but my lips wouldn't move. The guttural noises spilling from my mouth were confusing and animal-like, so I fell back asleep. I dreamt I was falling, falling, falling from a cliff, plunging into the murky swirling water of the Kentucky River . . .

I sat up.

Somewhere a bell rang loudly. A man with a military crew cut ran into the room and leaned toward me. He frightened me, so I tried pushing him away with my hands, but only my right hand would move and not in the direction I wanted.

*Who was this man? Was it O'nan? Were we still fighting? Were we falling off the cliff together? No, that was Sherlock Holmes falling off Reichenbach Falls with Moriarty.*

The strange man morphed into Basil Rathbone as he turned off a monitor. He was wearing a Key West T-shirt and shorts. A chuckle bubbled up my throat thinking of Sherlock Holmes in shorts. Sherlock turned toward the bed and smiled. There was a gap in his front teeth. Now, his face reminded me of Alfred E. Neuman's, but more exotic, more ethnic. I couldn't place why. His lips were moving and I concentrated to understand what he was saying.

*Why couldn't I hear him?*

"My name is Jacob Dosh. You can call me Jake. I am a physician's assistant. I'll be taking care of you," he said in loud, exaggerated tones. He held a silver pen light, which he kept flashing into my eyes. "You've had an accident, but you're all right. I need to check you. Understand? Nod yes, if that is okay." The man smiled and repeated what he had said – again and again.

It finally sank in. I nodded slightly.

His hands were warm and gentle, almost caressing as they moved about my body. There were calluses on his fingers and a raised scar down the length of his left forefinger.

My skin was extremely sensitive to touch.

I felt the vibrations of someone running into the room.

My daughter peered anxiously from the foot of the bed and then spoke to the man.

I whispered her name and tried to keep my head up, but sank back into the pillows. I mumbled, "Watson?" Sherlock and I were on a case in London.

Sherlock shook my shoulder again. "Hey, stay with us. Don't go back to sleep."

Struggling to keep my eyes open, I attempted to smile at my daughter but couldn't make my lips curl up.

"Well," said the man called Jake, checking my vital signs. "Who's Watson?"

My daughter grinned. "The sidekick to my mother's favorite beekeeper, Sherlock Holmes."

"Sherlock Holmes was a beekeeper?"

"He retired in Sussex Downs and kept bees. He wrote *The Practical Handbook of Bee Culture.*"

Jake scribbled on a chart and placed it on the end of the rented hospital bed. "I always thought Sherlock Holmes was a fictional character. I didn't know he was real."

My daughter waved to me. "Cut down on the morphine. She's ready to come back to the living."

But my daughter was wrong. I wasn't. I liked living in the dream world of Morpheus, believing I was safe, knowing that in real time, tragedy cannot be undone. Tragedy was a bucking horse. Sometimes you were able

to stay in the saddle and ride it out – sometimes not.
And I wasn't even prepared to put my foot in the stirrup.

# 2

My name is Josiah Reynolds and I'm a retired art history professor. I keep bees now and sell honey at the local Farmers' Market. I live in an iconic house called the Butterfly that was supposed to have been featured in *Architectural Digest* this spring. I guess that has been postponed. When I was flush with money, I collected Kentucky art and vintage movies.

Then my husband, Brannon, died and left all his money to his mistress, who was pregnant with his second child. He left his daughter and me nothing but a life insurance policy, hiding his wealth in secret accounts and what-nots. Because of it, I'm almost bankrupt. I didn't think things could get much worse until Richard Pidgeon, a honey competitor at the Farmers' Market, was murdered in my bee yard last fall, and then, I discovered that things could get much worse.

I now collect . . . trouble.

It was Hemingway who said, "The world breaks everyone. And afterwards many are strong in the broken places." It was because of Richard Pidgeon that I am now broken myself.

I pushed O'nan, the investigating cop, off a cliff because he was trying to kill me, but he pulled me over with him. He deserved it. I didn't.

I smashed into a limestone ledge forty feet below, while O'nan plummeted into the Kentucky River, which swallowed him. But that was after he shot my dog, Baby, and plugged a hole in Franklin, my friend. He did it because I got him pulled off the murder case of Richard Pidgeon, which he was trying to pin on me. I didn't kill Richard Pidgeon, but I know who did.

I don't like to discuss the details of my recovery, but it involved trips to Miami to visit plastic surgeons, dentists, innards doctors, ear doctors, brain doctors and leg doctors. I was poked, bled, stuck and scanned. I should have let O'nan just shoot me. It would have been less trouble for everyone.

Between the Miami trips were visits from physical therapists with their painful repetitive exercises. My face was ruined and, no matter how much therapy I endured, I would always walk with a pronounced limp. The fall had busted up my left ear but good, so I wore a hearing aid. My teeth were either broken or knocked out, so implants were installed but only after the wires for my broken cheekbone had been cut from the inside of my mouth. My beautiful red hair had to be shaved and had grown back gray. Not a pretty gray, but a lifeless dull color that reminded me of gristle. There's more wrong with me, but it is too technical to understand without a medical dictionary.

On top of that, I had slipped into a severe depression, and felt there was no need to spend money on doctors and therapists who couldn't really help anymore. Even Key West had lost its luster and the ocean no longer soothed. So you can imagine the fuss I put up when Jake informed me that several more months of therapy were needed before I could go home. Jumping Jehosaphat! I was done!

"Are you going to get out of bed today?" asked Jake, taking my pulse.

I shook my head.

"I need to make your bed," he said, tugging on the sheets.

"Lea tit," I mumbled. Now that the wires had been removed from inside my mouth, I could speak rather clearly if I took the time to enunciate carefully. I was still getting used to my new teeth. "'An I 'ave a fresh pain sot?"

"Nope, not time yet. We're trying to wean you off some of the pain medication."

"My doter gav instruckions . . . I was not . . . be in pain."

"Spoken like a true junkie."

19

"Blow tit tout ur ass," I said seething. I was tired of fighting the medical establishment for every hour of pain relief. Their constant harping on the amount of pain medication I was taking did not endear them to me, so I started to lie about it. They never cross-checked, but Jake knew the truth.

"Having a pity party all by yourself?" asked Jake. "You should be thankful that you're alive."

"Go soak 'our head."

"Ooooh whee. I sure understood that." He studied me for a moment. "Depression is part of the process, but you are taking it down to a whole new level. You're not thinking of doing something stupid, are you?"

I didn't reply.

"'Cause that would be like giving everyone the finger after all the time and money that's been invested to bring you back from the dead. I don't come cheap, which is why your poor daughter is sweating over a crummy case in Amsterdam so she can pay for all of this." He waved his hand around the room.

I gave him a raspberry, but in the process just deposited spittle on myself.

Jake pointed a rust-colored finger at me. "You're mad that she's not here, but she can't be." He lifted some pages on the bed chart and quickly read through them. "I am going to go against the doctor's advice here. I hope you don't get me in trouble with the medical establishment." He put down the chart. "Now don't kick or I'll drop you."

"Wat . . . 'ou doin'?"

"If the docs have their way, they'll just put you on more pills. I'm trying to get you off that crap. You need some vitamin D, so out in the sun you go." Jake lifted me, speaking like one gentling a spooked horse, and strode outside to where a small pool with pink tiling beckoned. Walking down the wide steps of the pool, Jake eased me onto a floating chair. As I was only dressed in a hospital gown, my fanny felt the free exposure to the water as Jake pried my hands from around his muscular neck. I shielded my eyes against the intense Florida sun. I felt naked, but then I almost was.

"Nothing to worry about. It's a beautiful day. Just relax and get some sun. And don't pee in the pool. I might want to take a swim later."

"Gonna pu sunscreen lotion on me?" I burned very easily, being a descendant of Vikings.

"Nope. I'll be back in fifteen."

"Jake, 'ou come back!"

He shut the glass doors to my bedroom, ignoring my pleas. Giving up my whining, I watched him put clean sheets on my bed. Finally checking his watch, he came out and jumped into the pool. After rubbing sunscreen on my arms and hairy legs, he placed a big straw hat on my head and handed me sunglasses. "That will keep you from burning. Now if you want out of this pool, you will have to take your flabby arms and paddle over to the shallow end. Once you do that, I'll come out to get you."

He pushed my chair into the deep end of the pool.

"I hate ur guts. 'Gonna repor' 'ou."

"Call me when you get to the shallow end. You gotta touch the rail."

I watched my jailer make four long cell phone calls from the patio. I counted them. "Who 'ou callin'?" I called out.

"None of your beeswax, missy. Now, if you push yourself to the end of the pool, I'll take you out to dinner. I'll dress you in a pretty muumuu and set you up in your new wheelchair and take you out for a spin. Whadja' say? I am bored stiff with my own cooking. Let's go out. If you behave, I'll watch one of those crappy old movies that you love so much after dinner."

He knew what I was thinking. "Your face doesn't look that bad. I've got some really strong makeup that will cover up those marks. I don't understand why you won't look in the mirror. It's really not that severe."

I took my time to speak clearly. "I'm jus not ready to see what I've 'come 'et. Understand?" I shyly fingered the red welts criss-crossing my face.

"A year from now those welts and cuts will be faded. You won't be able to tell that your face was injured."

I gave a Mona Lisa smile, which was all the movement that I was capable of at the moment, but I didn't believe Jake. But for his sake, I would try.

It took an hour and a half, but we finally made it to the restaurant on White Street. I had garlic mashed potatoes, applesauce and a virgin appletini through a long straw Jake brought with him.

To my surprise, I realized that I liked being pushed in a wheelchair and having people open doors for me. It made me think I was Lionel Barrymore in the movie *Key Largo*. I sure wasn't Lauren Bacall.

# 3

A few days later, I was doing my therapy of dog paddling around in the pool, as Jake had fired all the physical therapists, when Franklin casually sauntered out from the house and stood grinning at me. It took me a moment to recognize my friend who had been shot by O'nan that awful night of the policeman's attack. Yelping for joy, I made big splashes rushing toward him. "What 'ou doing here?" I was still having trouble with my y sounds.

He trudged down the pool steps, and after giving me a big sloppy kiss, said, "I went back to work too early and reinjured myself." He patted his shoulder. "I pulled something inside, so I am here to recuperate with you, if that's okay?"

"Okay? It's fantastic! What a wonnerful surprise." I pressed his hand against my cheek and then remembering my ruined face, pulled away.

Franklin took no notice. "I brought your mail. You've got tons of it – cards, letters, notes, even all the newspaper articles about what happened. Matt has saved every scrap of paper about us. We're famous. People buy me drinks at the bars. I got a bonus at work. I think it was a sympathy bonus, but who cares. It's money."

"I can't wait to ree all of tem, but tell me how are 'ou, really?"

"As well as can be expected. The bullet went through the soft tissue. No serious damage like . . . well, I'll heal okay. I had a cute doctor who flirted with me while I was in the hospital. Even Shaneika is sweet when she sees me."

"Did she bi 'er horse?"

"Oh, my gawd, is he a bruiser." Franklin playfully grabbed my arm, causing me to yelp. "Sorry there, old girl, I forgot. You're just put together with a little bit of glue and thread, aren't you."

"It's okay, Franklin. I'm doin' fine."

"Really? Because that Gestapo commandant who takes care of you called Matt, and said you were seriously depressed . . . like you might imitate a Norman Maine swim."

"Wouldn't tat be life im . . . tating art?"

"It would be life imitating *A Star Is Born* – every gay man's fantasy."

"No, just 'our gay Judy Garland fantasy," I laughed.

"Matt and I decided that you are going to die an ancient lady in bed with us watching you take your last gasp. Anything other than that, it is unthinkable. Besides where can Matt live where the rent is so great?"

"There is no rent."

"Like I said, where can he live where the rent is so great."

"'Ow's Matt?"

Franklin fingered the hem of the muumuu which I now wore every day, even when swimming. "Okay, I guess. He wallows in guilt, but I tell him there was nothing he could have done."

"Really?"

"Matt's not Matt anymore. He hardly talks to me. When he's not at work, which is eighty hours a week just about, he putters on that crappy cottage and your house – like frantic. Says he needs to fix everything before you come home."

"Want me to talk with him?" I asked, alarmed.

"No, please don't. Just get well, Josiah. Really well and come home. Then everything will work out."

I pounded on my legs in frustration. "If I just wasn't still in that chair, I could be of more use," I said, glancing at the wheelchair waiting patiently for me at the pool's edge.

"But ya are, Blanche. Ya are in that chair!" cried Franklin from the iconic scene in *What Ever Happened To Baby Jane.*

I made a face. "Have 'ou been waiting to use that line?"

"Ever since I knew you were in a wheelchair. Come on, you gotta admit it was a pretty good Bette Davis and you make a good Joan Crawford."

"It was scary."

"It was good."

"It was creepy."

"It sounded just like Bette Davis. Sorry, but did you lose your sense of play in the accident? Hmmmm? Was it yanked out of your ass by mistake?"

"Okay, Franklin. It was good. Just like Davis. Now, did 'ou bring honey from home?" I didn't want to explain that most things were not funny now. I was too busy waving off flashbacks of O'nan shooting my mastiff, Baby, and me falling off the cliff with him – screaming.

"Gobs and gobs of it. What are you doing with all that honey we keep sending?"

"Eat it. Put on my wounds. Helps me heal faster and lessens the scars."

"Isn't it sticky?"

"Bandages absorbs honey first . . . and think it's time bandages . . . changed." I looked around for Jake.

"No, wait. Josiah, I've got something else important to tell you." He gently held both my hands. "Now brace yourself. Did anyone talk to you about Baby?"

I stopped smiling. "Baby . . . never mentioned. Don't want to know."

"Well, I've got a good surprise for you. Let him go, Jake," called Franklin, watching my expression.

Jake nodded and smiling, opened the patio door, calling to someone inside. Out through the door lumbered something that looked like a bewildered, tawny lion.

"Call to him, Josiah," said Franklin. "Let him hear your voice."

"Ba . . . Baby?" I cried, my voice cracking. "Baby, Baby!" I looked toward Franklin. "But 'ow?"

Franklin didn't get a chance to explain as Baby turned to the sound of my voice and saw me struggling to get out of the pool. "Baby, come 'ere."

Recognition dawned on the mastiff as he sniffed the air. Hurrying to the side of the pool, he ferociously barked. Jake rushed to help me out of the pool, but Baby, ignoring his dislike of water, brushed Jake aside with his massive body, trying to climb down the pool steps. Rushing to meet him, I threw my arms around the thick neck of fawn fur and began to sob loudly. I cried as though a great stream of pain coursing through my body found an outlet through my eyes. I cried for all that I had been through – the murder investigation, the loss of my meager savings, that awful night when O'nan attacked and I fell with him over the cliff, the physical pain I had had to endure since then, my ruined body. I cried because I missed my late husband. I cried for Tellie, Richard's abused wife. I even cried for that jerk, Richard Pidgeon.

Through my hysterics, Baby patiently stood until I noticed his limbs were starting to quiver. "Sit, Baby, sit. Let me look at 'ou."

Baby gratefully sat with his massive tongue drooping from his mouth, drooling thick saliva on me.

I explored him with my hands and eyes. "Oh Baby," I sighed upon discovering his injuries.

Baby had only one good eye and an ugly scar creased the right side of his skull. Another scar marred his fur on the underside of his carriage. "'Ou lucky, lucky dog," I said, giving him another hug. I glanced fondly at Franklin. "He's so big."

"He weighs about one hundred fifty-five currently. Because of his injuries, the vet doesn't know if he'll reach the regular two hundred pounds. He limps somewhat, but the one eye doesn't seem to slow him down." Franklin rubbed Baby's massive head.

Baby turned his drooling tongue toward Franklin, licked him and slurped. He began panting in the hot Florida sun. Baby, not Franklin.

"You can thank Officer Kelly for saving Baby. Kelly was among the first cops to arrive and found Baby in the pantry. He got one of the paramedics to stabilize Baby until he could rush him to his own vet – a buddy of his. Josiah, Kelly has paid all of Baby's vet bills and kept him after he was released. He even took him to obedience school, but Baby doesn't know any commands cause he's dumb as a rock. Yes, he is. Yes, he is," Franklin said in baby talk, as he scratched Baby behind an ear.

Baby whimpered for more.

Franklin laughed. "You know how Kelly loves dogs, but he could never get Baby to bond with him." Franklin patted my shoulder. "Baby loves you, Josiah. He needs to be with you, so I brought him. Besides, he's eating the Kelly family into bankruptcy."

Franklin's statements only induced another wave of crying until an anxious neighbor called across the fence and asked if there was anything wrong.

Seeing that I was emotionally exhausted and wrung out, Jake ordered me to bed. He lowered it so Baby could climb on as well. Baby began licking his paws as I threw my arm over him. Usually restless with a few hours here and there of catnapping, I slept the sleep of angels until I awoke to the friendly patter of Jake and Franklin starting the grill. Baby's massive legs and paws hung over the bedside while he snored contently. I listened to Baby's soft grunts, the guys laughing and the rhythmic ebb and flow of the ocean's waves. I felt different – better, like something inside had been mended a tiny bit.

I could hope again.

# 4

The next four weeks I busted my butt movin' and groovin' to Jake's unconventional methods of physical therapy. He bought baseball gloves for us and I would catch the ball, or try to, sitting in my wheelchair stationed squarely in the little park down the end of our street. I had to wear a catcher's mask in case . . . well, I fumbled quite a bit. After several days, kids were joining us for our impromptu workout, leaving their computer games behind.

That particular therapy was accompanied by the game of throwing a shiny penny in the pool. This was Jake's idea of fun. He'd throw in a penny. I was to fall off my float, dive and get the penny. Nine out of ten times I couldn't get the coin, but Jake said that was okay. The therapy was in the struggle to get the penny.

What can I say? His methods seemed to be working and I wasn't bored.

When I had regained enough strength, Jake rented a
fishing boat and plunged me into the sea attached to a
floating harness contraption he had fashioned. If I
drifted too far from the boat, Jake would tug on the rope
attached to the harness and drag me closer. If I did well,
Jake would venture into deeper water the next day.

"Keep treading. Keep moving those legs!" he yelled
encouragingly, while munching on thick roast beef
sandwiches and slurping cold beer. Once he pulled me
out of the sea with one hand when a shark got a little too
close, then proceeded to drop me back in when it lost
interest and departed. I called Jake some pretty horrible
names. He just motioned for me to continue treading
while adjusting his Cardinals baseball cap against the
blazing sun.

Franklin would either join me snorkeling in the salty
water or stay onboard fishing with Jake. Time came
when Jake told me to pull myself on board. It took
twenty-five minutes and lots of profanity-laced grunts
before I managed to haul myself up and flop onto the
deck of the boat like a hooked fish. It took me another
fifteen minutes struggling to stand while Jake and
Franklin sat watching me, trading baseball statistics.

That was the day I took my first step since the
accident. That was the day I knew I was going to make it
back into the land of the living.

News of my recovery made its way back to Lexington.
Detective Goetz and the city's attorney, along with
Shaneika Mary Todd, my criminal lawyer, came to Key
West to take my deposition regarding my lawsuit against

the city. Goetz was all business as Shaneika watched over him like a sparrow hawk hovering over prey.

By that time, my memory had recovered for the most part and I gave a sound statement with only a few lapses.

The city's attorney kept asking the same questions over and over again until I complained of numbing weariness.

"You've got some pretty smooth explanations," said the city's attorney, his voice sounding like a repeating rifle.

"What do 'ou want me to do? Learn how to stutter," I seethed.

After that, their visit ended shortly, professional and somewhat disappointingly surreal. Goetz acted as though he didn't know me.

I was relieved when they left.

Eventually Franklin had to go back to Lexington, but not before many tears were shed by us both, not that Franklin would ever admit it to anyone.

But we would see each other soon. After all, there was only one month left to go on the lease at the Key West house.

\*

It was one of those rare cloudy days in Key West when Jake and I got back to the house. The sky was an unbroken canopy of wooly gray clouds. A smoky black line edging the horizon threatened a severe thunderstorm.

I had discovered a shop specializing in Haitian paintings and had purchased three for a song. It was all I could do to climb out of the cab with my new cane, one that Franklin had procured from an antique store while Jake carried my precious paintings, when I spied my Farmers' Market friend, Irene Meckler, sitting on the porch steps holding an overnight bag.

"For goodness sake, Irene," I called. "What are 'ou doing here?"

Irene rushed over, enveloping me in a warm hug. "I was just about to give up on you," she said smiling. "I've been waiting here for hours."

"Well, come on in. Are 'ou staying in a hotel?" I asked, spying her bag.

"You're going to think this forward of me, but I want to stay with you, Josiah."

"All right. This is Jake. He is . . . uhmm, my handyman."

Irene gave Jake the once over. "How handy is he, Josiah?" she asked rakishly.

Jake blushed and picked up Irene's bag after readjusting the paintings under his arms. "I'm her caretaker, so to speak. A physician's assistant." He grinned at me. "I make sure Mrs. Reynolds gets her medicine on time and doesn't drown in the pool – so I guess that is a type of handyman." He pointed some high-tech thingamabob that caused the front door to swing open.

"He will show 'ou to the guest bedroom and I will see 'ou at dinner. Sorry, dear, but I'm pooped. I need to rest now. We'll talk after dinner." We both waited silently as Jake went inside the house and returned a few minutes later, telling us we could enter.

"Handyman, huh," muttered Irene, following me inside the house.

"My casa, su casa," I said, ignoring her comment.

"Thank you, honey," said Irene gratefully. "I know this here's an inconvenience but I need . . ."

"No apologies, Irene. Just need a nap and then 'ou'll have my undivided attention."

Irene nodded and followed Jake down the hallway oohing and ahhing. She was right to make over the house. It was a darn beautiful house; light and airy inside while the outside exhibited exquisite landscaping with just the right amount of seediness to make it fit in with Key West.

I was in the middle of a long nap when Jake woke me. The sky looked very menacing and he wanted to eat before it rained.

It took me a while to dress, as I now had to do that myself. I stepped outside barefoot. Shoes were too much of a bother.

Dinner was served on the patio, and the three of us sat down to grilled yellowtail snapper topped with a cold cucumber dill sauce and fresh salad greens dressed with warm honey. Dessert was fresh raspberries over a bed of juicy sliced pears. Of course, my food had been pureed.

My gums were still very tender. Jake and Irene had wine while I sipped water spiked with lime juice. Jake put a maraschino cherry in my glass to dress it up.

Irene teased Jake that she would marry him if he would take charge of the household cooking.

"Why marry me then?" asked Jake. "Just hire me on as a cook."

"'Cause that way, I would have a lifelong interest in you," kidded Irene, laughing. Underneath the teasing, I thought Irene might be serious.

Jake cleared off the table. While he was in the kitchen, Irene leaned over and asked, "What is Jake?"

"Hey, Jake," I yelled over my shoulder. "What are 'ou?"

"Choctaw," replied Jake, poking his head out the kitchen door.

"'Ur people hunt in Kentucky back in the day?"

"Not unless there was a famine. Mostly Shawnee, Cherokees, some Wyandots hunted in Kentucky."

"I guess no one of 'ur ilk is named after Andrew Jackson."

"Nope, we pretty much hate his guts. Well, ladies, I am begging off for the night. See you in the morning."

Irene leaned over and whispered, "I hope we didn't embarrass him."

"Why should he be embarrassed about being a Choctaw? I don't get embarrassed if people ask me if I'm Scandinavian. I like talking about my ancestors. I'm sure he does too."

"Well, you know, the Indian Removal Act, the Trail of Tears. The fact that so many of them died during that winter."

"'Ou and I had nothing to do with that. I refuse to feel guilty about something that happened almost two hundred years ago. Should I feel guilty about what the Vikings did? Besides, every dog has his day and the Choctaws are making a killing with their casinos. Let's drop the subject, okay?"

"Why does he carry a gun with him?"

"Does he?" I replied.

"You know damn well he does. You can see it underneath his shirt. What's going on here? I think he is more than just a nurse's aide. Are you in trouble again, honey? I thought everything was over and done with."

Coming to my rescue, Baby lumbered over and placed his massive head in Irene's lap. "Josiah, get this monster off me. He's slobbering all over my skirt."

"Baby, lie down. Go on now. Lie down. Good boy. Good boy," I said.

Baby licked his jaws and the top of his nose before sneezing on Irene. As he shook his head, a long strand of thick, sticky drool fell on Irene's canvas shoes before he lumbered off to find Jake. Pursing her lips with considerable restraint, Irene said nothing as she glanced at her stained shoes.

I turned toward Irene. "Okay, let's have it. How did 'ou know where I was?"

"Everyone knows where you are," replied Irene, pushing up her glasses a nose so thin at the ridge it looked like it could cut paper. "You can't keep a secret like that in a small town like Lexington very long."

Seeing the confused look on my face, she said, "Matt has been sending out your mail from the Keene post office thinking he was being real sneaky. Well, golly, Josiah, Keene's only got one building – the store that attaches onto the post office. Don't you think someone that looks like Matt would be noticed? Women started driving by all hours of the day hoping they could catch a glimpse of him. It's not every day you see someone that looks like Antonio Banderas in the flesh. To make a long story short, Miriam, the peach lady, lives in Keene and just went in one day while he was there and looked over his shoulder, so to speak. All the packages were addressed here in Key West. Then the funny little guy that got shot with you came back to town with a tan. When he wouldn't tell anyone where he had been, we all assumed he was with you. So – here I be."

"Victor Mature."

"Huh?"

"Matt looks like Victor Mature." I took a sip of my lime drink. "Okay, I've got the how. Now, let's hear the why."

Irene bowed her head. "I feel bad asking you since you're still recuperating, but I've got no one else to turn to."

I reached over and clutched Irene's hand. "My daughter told me that 'ou came or called every day that I was in the hospital, and that 'ou cooked for her. A person can't have too many friends like that, Irene. If there is something that I can do for 'ou, I will try."

Irene lifted her glasses and wiped the tears away that threatened to spill down her pinched features. "It's my sister's boy – Jamie. You've met him?"

"Once or twice."

"He's dead, Josiah. Drowned in the river."

"I'm so sorry, Irene. When did this happen?"

"Over two weeks ago. They say he drowned, but there's something that just ain't right about his death. He was on the river late at night. My sister has no explanation for what he was doing on the water after midnight. And the coroner said there was gasoline residue on his clothes."

I remained still while Irene caught her breath.

"To make matters worse, that same night, the Golden Sun Vineyard caught on fire. Someone torched fire to their vines . . ."

"So 'ou think that Jamie set fire to the vineyard, and as he was making his escape, he had an accident and drowned?" I interrupted.

Irene shrugged.

I paused. It took me longer now to collect my swirling thoughts and make sense of them. I know it was unsettling for people to sit together in silence. It's considered rude, but since the accident, my mind was a machine slow in the processing of information. Irene waited patiently.

"This Golden Sun Vineyard . . . isn't this the winery that claims that they have discovered the heritage grape that served as Thomas Jefferson's table wine and was the site of the first commercial winery in the United States?"

"Yes," replied Irene peevishly, "but we all know that my sister's vineyard, the Silver Creek Vineyard, was the first in the United States."

"Now don't get huffy, Irene," I said, "but I read in the paper that the Golden Sun Vineyard can prove their claims with journals, old deeds and letters. Did those claims worry your sister? Be honest."

"It worried her a touch. People would think that she was lying all those years."

"She based her claims on oral history and legend which, unfortunately, is sometimes inaccurate. But if that is all 'ou've got to go on, no one can fault her for making those claims." My left hand began to twitch, which it now does when I am tired. "Still, I don't see how I can help, Irene."

"You know people, Josiah. You have resources that my sister and me don't. You know how the system works after what you went through with Richard Pidgeon's death. I know it's a lot to ask, but if you could just look into it when you get back home, I'd be much obliged. I'm a-tellin' you, Josiah, something in my bones tells me that boy was murdered."

Observing Irene's fervor, I nodded, but privately I didn't know what I could do. I could barely walk.

Coming to my rescue, Jake poked his head out from his bedroom and called, "Boss Lady, time for bed."

I looked apologetically at Irene. "We'll pick this up tomorrow, Irene. I'm very tired. I'm still building up my strength."

"Of course. Do you need help?"

"Nope, this is part of my therapy. I now have to get ready for bed on my own. Jake has a monitor in my room, so if I fall, he can hear me." I tugged on the muumuu. "And everything is kept together with velcro. Jake's idea. I have to work my way up to buttons and zippers."

Whatever thoughts Irene had as she watched me limp to my bedroom, she kept to herself.

I awoke around two in the morning to catch Irene sitting in the same patio chair.

A storm had cut loose and was raining heavy sheets of silvery droplets.

Irene's silhouette played against the reflection of the pool on the property's pink stucco wall. Streaks of bright lightning illuminated her calmly smoking, while watching the night sky from the protection of the covered patio.

Sighing, I pushed Baby over to the side of the bed, away from my spine.

He didn't even flinch.

All the bedroom doors opened on to the patio.

I heard Jake get up from his bed, peep in my door and then check on Irene. They spoke and then he went back to his room. His mattress squeaked as he climbed back in bed. Within minutes an occasional snore sounded from his room. It seemed that only the women were beset by worries.

Over the next several days, I pumped Irene for information concerning her nephew while we went sightseeing around the island. After extending our walks a little more each day, Irene would bring me home by taxi, so I could take a long nap and then finish my pool therapy. After dinner, I was ready for bed. While we occupied ourselves, Jake made arrangements to close the house and to transport Baby and me back to Kentucky.

On the last day of her visit, Irene pulled me into a brightly painted beauty shop on Catherine Street in the Cuban section of Old Town. There were pictures of the Madonna on the mirrors at every station and old black and white snapshots of a young Cuban woman standing in a deserted Paseo del Prado in Havana or with the El Morro Fortress in the background, smiling and waving at the person taking the picture.

"Josiah, I don't want to fuss, but you need to have your hair done. You shouldn't go back to Kentucky looking like . . . well, like you do." She played with my hair, which was three inches long in some areas, four inches in others along with a bald patch here and there. "I've made arrangements for a total make-over and I'm gonna pay for it. That's the least I can do for you. I've 'splained everything to this here lady."

I started to protest, but Irene motioned toward a grim-looking woman who gently took me by an arm and deposited me into her chair. I looked again at the snapshots and determined the older beautician working on my hair and the young girl in the picture were one and the same.

Irene, with her Kentucky country accent, and the Spanish-speaking woman prattled like old friends, both obviously disgusted with my appearance. The Cuban lady tsk-tsked while Irene clucked like an old hen when discussing my hair. Irene dug out an old photo of us together from her purse and negotiated the color of my hair with the beautician.

The beautician nodded and her work began in earnest.

I couldn't stand to look in the booth mirrors, so I pretended to be asleep for most of the time. My eyebrows were waxed and chin hairs plucked first. Then the work on my head began. My hair was colored, trimmed and styled. A hot solution of bath oils soaked my raggedy-looking feet. Afterwards toenails were painted, as were my fingernails.

After several hours, Irene said, "Let's put some make-up on her." Before I could open my mouth to protest, Irene said, "Shut up, Josiah. This is my party."

I slumped down in my chair yielding to exhaustion. It was past my naptime. Finally, I heard, "Josiah, open your eyes and look in the mirror. Trust me."

After seven months of deliberately not looking at myself, I opened my eyes to a three-paneled mirror. The woman before me had a jaunty spiked haircut of golden red hair. Her green eyes stood out against the dark eyeliner and bronze makeup. I touched my cheek. No – that wasn't makeup. That was a tan. I felt my jaw line and brow. I lifted my hair to see the telltale signs of plastic surgery. My fingers lingered on the fading welts,

Scratches, and surgeon's cuts. I sat back in my chair and stared at the woman in the mirror before me.

"Everything lines up," I gushed breathlessly.

"Yep, they did a good job putting you back together. Nothing seems out of kilter. They even matched up your eyeball sockets."

"I have cheekbones," I said.

"That's cause you've lost so much weight, they stand out. If you lost more of that belly flab, you'd be a stunner."

I gaped into the mirror at a woman I hadn't seen for many years. "Irene, do I look 'ounger to 'ou?"

"Like you did when I first met you." Irene chuckled. "Your daughter told the surgeons, while they were working on you, to make you look younger. That girl never misses an opportunity. I was there when she told them, 'now don't make her look too young, just younger.'"

Laughter gurgled up my throat and escaped into delighted hoots. "Oh my gawd!" I cried ecstatically. "I thought I looked like the hunchback of Notre Dame. I actually look presentable. What a freaking relief!"

The Cuban hairdresser started speaking to me in Spanish, which I don't understand but it didn't take a translator for me to realize that she was happy too. "Good lady," I said, "thank you. Thank you."

Irene helped me out of the chair and we walked out of the tiny little beauty parlor with the Cuban lady chatting merrily behind us. She called to people in the street, who strolled over to take a good gander at me. One middle-aged man gave me a thumbs-up before joining his buddies playing chess across the street. Several matrons reached up and rearranged my bangs during a heated debate with the hairdresser. She pushed them away and taking a comb out of her apron, gave my hair a final pat.

Jake was waiting with a cab. He did a double take and then broke out into a broad grin. When he saw tears in my eyes, Jake gave me a big hug. "I told you it wasn't that bad. The docs did a good job on you."

I let Jake help me into the cab while Irene dug in her big purse for a handkerchief. I ruined my eye makeup blubbering all the way home.

After giving me a final once-over, Irene declared me fit for society and that she could go home satisfied. A day later, she left on a commuter plane bound for Miami, but not before she laid her hands on my head and gave me her blessing. "And Jacob was left alone; and a man wrestled with him until the breaking of day. When the man saw that he did not prevail against Jacob, he touched the hollow of his thigh; and Jacob's thigh was put out of joint as he wrestled with him. Then he said, 'Let me go.' But Jacob said, 'I will not unless you bless me.' And he said to him, 'What is your name?' And he said, 'Jacob.' Then he said, 'Your name shall be Israel for you have striven with God and with men and have prevailed.'"

"In other words, keep the faith, baby."

"Keep on keeping on, Josiah. It's all we can do. See you in Lexington."

A week later I boarded a rented RV with Jake, Baby, my new paintings, lots of hair dye and a driver heading for Kentucky. I counted every mile marker going home as I craved to walk on the sacred hunting grounds of the Shawnee.

I also had a mystery to solve.

# 5

We turned onto the gravel driveway that divided two mowed pastures with new plank fences. Bluebird boxes nailed to the fence posts sparkled with blue-pink flashes of hurrying nesting pairs rushing back and forth. Past the bird boxes, into the left pasture grazed a stallion whose coat gleamed blue-black in the spring sunlight. He stared at the passing RV before contemptuously galloping to the far side by jumping across the stream that divided the field, his black mane and tail fluttering in the wind. A couple of nanny goats trotted after him.

In the other pasture grazed several old racers that had been rescued from the butcher's block. They good-naturedly raced the RV the length of their field.

The redbuds, their full, pink glory fading, were accented by the white blooms on the dogwood trees as they were beginning to reveal their flowers in the patch of woods beyond the clearing.

The last time I had been home, the leaves had been turning orange.

We slowly passed the old 'baccer cure barn that nestled in a once-neglected tobacco field which had been recently tilled. It was freshly painted black with a bright quilt square of a star blazing its forehead. Missing planks had been replaced and weeds cut from around the base of the early twentieth-century relic. From inside the open doors of the barn peeped a new tractor. A llama and her new baby, several feral cats along with a flock of wild turkeys, using the barn as a base, scurried to the woods upon sighting the RV.

My, my, but Matt and Shaneika had been busy in my absence. The RV rattled past Matt's shack, which had been painted dark green with sea green shutters and door. A shiny metal roof graced the top. New patio furniture sat on the front porch and several flowerbeds had been excavated, waiting patiently for their new occupants. Japanese maple trees, Kentucky bamboo and ornamental birch trees lay casually strewn, still in their burlap balls. I could see Matt had plans for my little cottage.

The dusty gravel road gave way to the more expensive pea gravel that had been raked into a wavy pattern. We turned the bend and there stood my house, the Butterfly, but not as I had left her. Water thundered down from her middle copper gutter making a spectacular waterfall splash creating a small rainbow at its granite basin. The windows winked back with shimmering clean glass. The flowerbeds were raked free from years of debris with new native plants and trees freshly planted. The house's limestone and wood looked as though it had been power washed for it was free of weather and age stains. The Butterfly looked brand new.

"Man oh man," whistled Jake. "This is some house."

"I haven't see the Butterfly look this good since she was built." I clapped my hands together. "Oh, she's a grand old lady."

When the RV stopped by, I had to wait until Jake let me down the handicap lift with Baby wagging his tail beside me.

One of my daughter's overly-muscled minions opened the front alcove door.

Baby growled and leaned against me, putting pressure on my bad leg. I patted him reassuringly while trying to shift his weight.

"Good afternoon, Mrs. Reynolds. I trust you had a pleasant trip. My name is Cody and I'll be assisting you until your daughter returns. There have been some security changes. I will explain those after you've had a chance to rest." He exchanged glances with Jake, and then went to help the driver retrieve our luggage.

"Cody?" I murmured to Jake. "Sounds like he's named after a horse."

"Don't underestimate him. Cody's very good."

I limped through the bamboo alcove and passed through the double steel doors. I paused in the foyer, inhaling the house's new odors.

She smelled from the damp of the river, Chanel No. 5 and fresh paint.

As I roamed the rooms, lyrics from the *Wizard of Oz* "*can you even dye my eyes to match my gown*" – from when Dorothy and her compatriots first entered the wondrous Emerald City – wouldn't leave my head. I began humming the tune. I was just as enthralled with what I saw, as had been the tin man, scarecrow and lion. And just like me, the Butterfly had had an overhaul.

New polished riverbed limestone counters graced the kitchen. The backsplash was inlaid with Kentucky agate. The house's inside concrete walls had been freshened while the classic '50s and '60s furniture, sprinkled here and there with antiques, had been steamed, cleaned or polished. My treasured Nakashima table was burdened with a dramatic flower arrangement of birds of paradise. In fact, large flower arrangements in huge glass vases graced all the living areas. My art collection had been rehung and ceiling lights installed to highlight the most dramatic pieces. I counted the paintings. Uh oh. Some were missing.

I spotted my art glass collection and smiled. Stephen Powell had fixed his piece and returned it. It was standing by itself on an eighteenth-century dough table by a window. For a moment the sight of it reminded me of my struggle with O'nan and I felt chilled, but the piece seemed to reach out to comfort me with its startling beauty. I limped over to examine it. I couldn't tell where it had been damaged. Good. But I didn't like it on the dough table. Somewhere in the house was a column with a built-in light box that illuminated from the bottom up. That would really bring the piece to life, but I didn't see it. Maybe O'nan had broken it during his rampage. I would think about that tomorrow. "After all, tomorrow is another day," I whispered to myself, mimicking Scarlett O'Hara's voice.

I showed Jake the guest room and bath. It had been completely redone with new paint, drapes and bedspread. Jake placed his luggage on the bed and opened the glass door, stepping out onto the back patio. Sensing that he wanted to be alone, I closed his door, knowing that he must be exhausted from the trip. He had kept vigil while I slept most of the way home.

While Jake took in his new surroundings, I hobbled to my bedroom. The room had been redone in soft blues and greens. My Hans Wegner twin beds had been pushed together to make one large bed while white faux fur rugs covered the floor. Cheerful Jesta Bell landscapes adorned the walls. Somehow they fit with the austere Danish modern furniture. In the corner sat a blond '50s vanity set complete with my brushes, perfume and toiletries. The dark gray slate floors had been buffed to a soft sheen. It was the right mixture of elegance and kitsch.

"I think I've died and gone to heaven," I murmured to Baby. "Oh, Baby, look. You have your own bed." A large dog bed lined with fake mink was placed next to mine. "We're living at the Ritz now," I kidded, patting his massive head.

Baby swallowed a substantial amount of drool and looked at me with his eyebrows arched. He sniffed the dog bed as though knowing it was meant for him.

"How much did this cost and who paid for it?" I whispered to myself.

Large new colored glass tiles with a water wave pattern in the bathroom replaced the brown and orange '80s tiles, which had been popping out for the past two years. The chipped tan sink was replaced with a blue-green glass bowl and all new faucets had been installed as well as handicap bars and a land phone.

A huge flat-screen TV sat opposite my bed. Underneath, a mini refrigerator was discreetly hidden along with my movie collection. My mind swirled.

As I opened the patio door, a honeybee immediately flew past my face. Lots of honeybees flitted around the pool with the intention of getting a drink of water. Their water tank must be empty. I would check on them tomorrow. One landed on my arm. I brought her up to my face for inspection, looking for mites or misshapen wings. She stared back and then shook her pollen-covered body before flying off.

Tears threatened to spill onto my face. I had endured the darkest winter of my life, worse than the death of my husband. But I had survived. Not better, not even whole, but somewhat intact. So had my bees.

Under the warm sun, the bees hummed along the patio searching for bright flickering colors, which signified flowers moving in the breeze to their compound eyes. Occasionally, they used me as a platform where they could rest while brushing pollen from their furry bodies into the pollen baskets on their hind legs.

Stepping outside and kicking off my bedroom slippers, I gazed at the turquoise sky while drawing strength from the earth, through my clothes, through my skin deep into my muscles, through my bare feet on the dirt. An occasional red-tailed hawk drifted overhead. As the wind lifted the hawk, it carried the sounds of the humming of insects, the calls of red-winged blackbirds, the chattering of gray squirrels, dogs howling on a faraway farm, Angus cattle mooing and the occasional cries of peacocks. An American goldfinch flittered past, his feathers turning from winter olive green to bright summer yellow. The droning of the bees almost lulled me to sleep.

Reluctantly I went back in, waving goodbye to my sisters – the bees.

I was home.

# 6

The next morning I commandeered Jake to drive down the dirt road to the Kentucky River dock that I shared with Lady Elsmere, my next-door neighbor. There I kept a rusty old fishing boat which Brannon and I had used to motor up and down the river bird-watching. Tied next to my boat was a new luxury party pontoon boat, which had been recently purchased by Lady Elsmere, aka June Webster from Monkey's Eyebrow, Kentucky.

I stood on the dock, looking at my dirty johnboat filled with last fall's leaves and its hard flat seats. My head swiveled to glance at the luxurious cushioned captain seats on the pontoon boat. I stared at my leaky johnboat with a puddle of water on the floor. My head turned to study the carpeted floor on the new shiny pontoon boat with its sunroof. I looked again at the johnboat with its mildewed lifejackets hanging off the dented aluminum sides. The pontoon boat had sturdy side rails and convenient cup holders built into the seating. It also had a plank, which would be easy for me to board from the dock.

I decided to "borrow" Lady Elsmere's new boat. I knew she would keep the key in a canvas bag stashed in a hole on a sycamore tree near the water's edge. It was where we kept all our river valuables.

Delighted that he had access to a boat again, Jake happily installed me in a seat, put a life jacket on me, checked the gas and started the motor. Carefully he pulled away from the dock while I chatted about the unique ecosystem of the Palisades and the Bluegrass Region, which was on the World Monuments Fund's list of the one hundred most endangered sites because of the ticky-tacky development that central Kentuckians had allowed to occur.

Jake learned of Daniel Boone's land grant claim of one thousand acres in his daughters' names between East Hickman Road and the village of Spears. The location of his cabin was not too far from the river. Ol' Daniel must have spent much time on the river near the Devil's Pulpit, a sixty-foot rock formation we were passing which he noted in 1770. It is a freestanding stone column from which the Devil taunts passersby.

I prattled on about local history until we eventually pulled into a dock on the Madison County side of the river. Jake steadied the boat as I climbed out and then he had to fish out my cane, which I had inadvertently dropped into the river. Now with wet cane firmly in hand and Jake on the other side, I limped the short distance to the Silver Creek Vineyard tasting room.

As efficiently as ever, Jake whipped out the abuterol spray, which I needed for my wheezing. Apparently my body's protesting its lack of oxygen was disturbing to the other customers, who looked darkly in my direction. I inhaled my drug and smiled sweetly at the staring visitors. "Sorry, just a touch of viral TB," I said. They quickly averted their eyes. I sat at a table away from them.

A server with a tray of wine glasses containing different wines wound his way to our table.

Jake asked for Mrs. Dunne. "Tell her that Josiah Reynolds is here, please."

Several minutes later, a petite woman with short blond hair hurried to my table while wiping her hands on a chef's apron. Jake pulled out a chair for her and then excused himself to take a walk in the vineyards.

Sarah gave me the once over. "It seems, Josiah, that you have had a bad time of it," she said, noticing my cane and hearing aid.

"It would seem that we both have had a bad time lately."

"Well, thank you for coming, though I don't know what you can do. Irene's got some crazy notion that my boy's death wasn't an accident."

"What do 'ou think?"

She shook her head. "I don't know what to think. I do have questions – like what was he doing on the river so late at night, and why did he have gasoline on his clothes? It just doesn't make sense to me."

"What do 'ou think I can do?"

"Josiah, you know lots of people who will talk to you. I thought about hiring a private detective, but you know river people around here won't talk to a stranger." She shook her head as though trying to awaken from a nightmare. "I just want some answers." Looking at me with grief-stricken brown eyes, she pleaded. "I want closure, I guess."

I understood how the death of a loved one plagued the living, especially if there was discord or unanswered questions. It was our nature as humans to put things in their rightful places, to tidy up our relationships before we could part with them. Otherwise we spent our time thinking, "could have, should have, if only I had done this or that." It could drive a person nuts dreaming of alternate endings.

"How old was 'our boy?"

"Fifteen, almost sixteen, but he looked much older. He was big for his age."

"Did he often go out onto the river at night?"

"Not that I am aware of, but he did spent a great deal of time on the river – kayaking, tubing, fishing. He loved the outdoors and water. He swam quite a bit by the dock."

I shuddered. I loved the river too, but thinking of swimming with water snakes gave me the heebie-jeebies. I loved the river just fine from inside a boat.

"How can 'ou explain the gas on his shirt?"

Sarah's eyes lowered. "I don't know," she replied. For the first time, I sensed that she was lying.

"Wasn't there a fire at the Golden Sun Vineyard that night?"

"Yes, but gosh, that's almost half an hour from here by boat. In a kayak, it would take much longer as coming back Jamie would have to paddle against the current."

"But 'our boy was very strong and big for his age?"

"Yes," she said after hesitating.

"I understand that they are making a solid claim of being the first commercial vineyard in the United States and that Henry Clay and Thomas Jefferson had stock in the company."

Sarah nodded her head. "They've found some documents that support that claim."

"Has that hurt your business?"

"Well," she shrugged, "I don't know for sure. My sales are down, but that could just be the economy. I do know that they are the shiny new toy in the wine industry. But Ian Peterson, who owns Golden Sun, wants to do a riverboat tour this summer from his winery and include Silver Creek in it as well. I thought it was a great idea. If anything, my food sales would go up with the increased traffic."

I thought for a moment. "Sarah, I can't promise anything, but I'll ask around." I pointed to my cane, "and I sure can't do this in a hurry. It may be some months before I can get any information."

"That's okay. My boy is not going anywhere," she said wistfully.

I squeezed her hand. "That's for sure. Before I go, can 'ou give me a list of his friends and their phone numbers?"

"Sure, no problem. Also, the house is open. If you wish, go see his room before you leave."

"That would be good." I watched Sarah leave. She had two other children, but they were grown and gone. Jamie was her baby.

As Sarah scurried to gather a list for me, I carefully negotiated the stone pathway to her house and entered through the back door. The house was unusually tidy for a woman who worked sixty hours a week at her own business. Sarah had to keep house, run the winery, cook for the lunch crowd and special dinners, and tend the vines while managing the rest of the farm, which also grew vegetables for local restaurants. I knew she had help, but there was still a lot on her plate.

Fortunately, the house was a ranch and I meandered through the hallway looking for Jamie's room where I suddenly bumped into a young girl with a bucket of cleaning products in her hands backing out of a room. We both jumped and screamed. Spying my cane, she decided I must be a lost tourist.

"GAWD, you scared me!" she exclaimed.

"Sorry. I should have called out. Mrs. Dunne told me the house was open, but she didn't mention 'ou. I'm looking for Jamie's room."

She jerked a stained thumb over her shoulder. "I don't clean his room. Mrs. Dunne don't like nobody in't."

"Well, I am glad to see that she has help. Have 'ou worked here long?"

"Yes, ma'am. For two years. I was in Jamie's class. That's how I got the job. He suggested me to her."

"Were 'ou two close?"

She blushed. "No, nothing like that. He just knew I needed a job bad and mentioned me to his mom. Jamie was thoughtful like that."

"My name is Mrs. Reynolds. 'Ou are?"

"Bloomie. Bloomie Lamb. I live up the road from here." She pulled a wisp of dirty blond hair away from her sweaty broad-cheeked face. Although young, Bloomie had known a life of hard work. Her hands were callused and rough looking, while her nails were cut short for working. Her accent was of the mountains. She stood looking expectantly at me.

"Did Jamie go out on the river much late at night?"

"If he was night fishing, he would. He would have to borrow a boat. His kayak wouldn't be right for that."

"Doesn't his mother have a boat?"

"Yeah, she's got a nice fishing boat, but locks it up at dark. She'd never have let him use it 'cause it's dangerous on the river at night." She pointed west. "Up for miles ain't no houses, no lights. It'd be hard to see unless there was a full moon, plus all sorts of critters roam the

Palisades at night. Some even say painters are making a comeback. They've heard their screams."

I smiled at her use of painter – a mountain word for big cat. "Yes, I've heard that panthers might be back in the region." I wanted to change the subject. "What about a life jacket? No one has mentioned if he was wearing one."

"He rarely used them. Jamie could swim like a fish."

"Whose boat would he borrow?"

"Sometimes a friend from up river; sometimes, Mr. Meckler, his uncle."

"It sounds like you're saying he would go out at night without his mother knowing about it?"

"Jamie didn't need much sleep. His was a restless nature."

I didn't add that she was being evasive. "Did Jamie have any special female friends?"

"Like a girlfriend?" She blushed.

I nodded.

"No ma'am. Jamie did three things in his life . . . school, work and the river."

"Did he have any special buddies?"

Bloomie looked at me sideways. "No ma'am. He had lots of friends, but nobody the way you mean. Jamie was a good boy, smart. We had biology and English together. He was a good student, not top of the class, but still smart."

"Any sports?"

Bloomie started to move past me. I could tell she was getting uneasy with all the questions. "No ma'am. Like I said, he had to work all the time. If you don't mind, I best be gittin' back to my chores. His room's the last on the left."

"Thank 'ou, Bloomie. I'm much obliged that 'ou took the time to talk with me."

She shot me a quick forced smile before hurrying down the hallway. The back door slammed shut on her way out.

I slowly pushed the door open to Jamie's room. It was a typical bedroom for a boy of fifteen, almost sixteen. There were posters of Slash and Beckham. Also put in a place of honor over his bed was a vintage poster of Farrah Fawcett in a red bathing suit along with one of the Dixie Chicks.

So Jamie liked thin blondes. That left out Bloomie with her thick waist, snub nose and broad peasant face.

I eased down on the bed and studied Jamie's belongings. Pulling his backpack onto the bed, I went through his notebooks and schoolbooks. Nothing. No weird drawings or doodling. No self-destructive ramblings. Just finished homework assignments. I quickly went through all his drawers. Nothing appeared unusual. I stood in the middle of the room flummoxed.

"Boss Lady, you done?" asked Jake, poking his head in the room.

"Jumping Jehosaphat, 'ou scared the stuffing out of me!"

"YOU!" Jake admonished. "You scared the stuffing out of me. I see we still need to work on your y's."

Ignoring his comment, I asked, "When *you* were a boy, where did *you* hide things from your mother?"

"Much better. Umm, I'd hide things under the mattress."

"Can 'ou . . . you check for me?"

"Sure thing." Jake got on his knees and deftly felt under the mattress. Seeing something, he crawled underneath the bed frame, emerging with two raunchy magazines. Jake's lips puckered as he perused them. "He sure liked his hanky-panky hard core. This stuff even embarrasses me. Lots of S & M images here. I don't think a normal fifteen-year-old boy would gravitate to this stuff unless he was twisted."

"Give me those things. His mother doesn't need to know about this." I put the magazines in a pillow sham that had been thrown in a corner.

Jake reached under the bed again and pulled out an empty condom wrapper. "It seems like our boy liked his pleasures."

I held the sham open for the wrapper. "Can you check his closet while I search his desk?"

Jake did a quick and dirty job of searching the closet while I took my time going through the papers in his desk and feeling under the drawers. He found a dusty bag of grass. Jake smelled it. "Old. Stale. Not a serious smoker." Taking note of my feeling under the desk, Jake checked the mirror and pulled drawers from the bureau. "What are we looking for?" asked Jake.

"I don't know. Something that doesn't fit. Something unusual."

"What about the bathroom?"

"He had to share with the rest of the house. Only his mother has a private bath."

"Where's his computer?"

"Computer's over at the wine tasting room, used only for business."

"Cell phone?"

"I will double-check, but I think not. I don't think the Dunnes have the money for such toys . . . didn't see the need for them. I think Mrs. Dunne is old-fashioned about the use of new technology."

I sat in a chair with my head resting on my cane, scanning the room. "What doesn't fit?" I asked myself softly. My eyes slid to the walls. "Jake, can you press on Lady Farrah? I bet our boy hid secret stuff behind her smile."

"Would love to. Excuse me, Miss Fawcett, but I have to feel you up. Hope you don't mind," he said, as he pressed his hands against the poster.

I frowned.

"Hey, be pleased I didn't say grope. Wait a minute. What do we have here?" asked Jake as he slid out a newspaper article and a map from behind the poster.

"What does it say?"

Jake read it quickly and looked at the map. He handed them to me. "It's an article about the Golden Sun Vineyard and their claim of being the site of the first commercial winery in the country. He's got red circles around paragraphs."

"And this is a map of their place if one went down the river. Look – Jamie even marked the route with a pen. I think we better take this."

"What do you think, Boss Lady?"

"The same as you, Jake. I think there is a link between the poster, the magazines and the dope. Possibly the person who gave Jamie the Farrah Fawcett poster is the same person who supplied the raunchy magazines and possibly the condoms. You are right, Jake, about those magazines. They are too nasty for a fifteen-year-old boy unless he's bent, and no way would he be allowed to purchase them. Besides, they are very old magazines, the same vintage as the Fawcett poster. Since he hid the article behind the Fawcett poster, it indicates to me that Jamie wanted to keep his thoughts about the Golden Sun secret from his mother as well as the porn. It's only a theory but at least it's a start. I'm going to ask Sarah about the adult men in Jamie's life. I know that a woman would never have given him that trash."

"Maybe he found this stuff?"

"Where? No other houses are around so he wasn't trash snooping. Besides, the magazines look almost new and they are the same age as the Farrah Fawcett poster. They've been carefully treated, as if preserved by a collector. I think they are from the same person."

With that, we heard the door open. Jake quickly threw the pillow sham out the window.

A few seconds later, Sarah strode into the room.

"Did you find anything?" she asked.

"Found this behind the Fawcett poster," I said, showing her the newspaper article and the map.

"Oh dear," Sarah replied, looking at the article.

"Mind if I take this with me?"

"No, be my guest."

Struggling to rise from my chair, I said, "We'll be going now. Oh, by the way, Sarah, who were the adult men in Jamie's life . . . someone like an uncle or a mentor?"

"Well, there's Irene's husband. He and Jamie go fishing all the time . . . or did." She paused, staring at Jamie's things in haunted disbelief. I patted her arm in sympathy, causing her to regain her composure. "He and Irene were always good to my children, especially after my husband passed away." She pondered for a moment. "Then there was our youth minister from church in Richmond, Ison Taggert. Jamie really liked him."

"Who gave Jamie the Farrah Fawcett poster?"

Sarah smiled at the poster. "Ison Taggert. He was going to throw it out, so Jamie asked for it. Looks pretty innocent now, doesn't it."

"She certainly is hot," commented Jake.

Sarah and I turned to glare at him.

Jake, seeing our disapproval, said he would wait for me outside. He hurried out of the room.

"One last thing, Sarah. Was Jamie sexually active?"

Sarah paled. "Of course not. He was only fifteen. Why do you ask?"

"Just trying to get a complete picture."

"Well, you get *that* picture out of your head. Jamie was a good boy. Never a moment's trouble to me. I mean, I purposely didn't have cable or let him have unlimited access to the computer just so I could keep his mind clean. He was never allowed to see movies with explicit sex or violence. I raised a wholesome boy."

I didn't want to get into a fight with Sarah about raging teenage hormones, so I made a quick retreat after thanking her. I didn't want her to see that I was irritated. I hated it when people asked for favors and then got annoyed with me for being thorough. Besides I wasn't feeling well. My leg was beginning to ache. Still – I didn't realize what was to come later that night.

\*

I filed away the sex magazines and other items in a cardboard box. Lowering my head to my desk, I felt faint and slightly nauseous. My leg was throbbing and itching while the rest of my left side ached. Even my gums were pulsating. I called for Jake. No response. He might be exercising in the pool, for it was his regime to swim thirty laps every day. Usually he had me do my therapy at the same time, but today I just begged off. I was too tired after the trip to the winery. It was too much too soon.

Limping into his room, I called his name. Not there. Opening the cabinet where he kept my medication, I searched for a pain patch or pills. Not finding one, I began to rummage through the various bottles until I became nearly hysterical. Where was all my pain medication?

"What are you doing?"

I turned around to see Jake lounging against the patio door, drying off with a towel. His torso was very muscular and sinewy. Like most Native Americans, he had little body hair.

"I'm looking for my pain medication, but I can't find it." I turned back to the cabinet and continued to rummage.

"You're not due another patch until tomorrow morning, Boss Lady."

"I know," I snapped, "but I need one now. The one I've got is not doing anything."

"That's because you over-exerted yourself today and then wouldn't do your therapy to stretch your muscles. It was bound to bunch them up and now you hurt."

"Damn it to hell!" I said, raising my voice, "I don't give a crap why I hurt. I just do. I need something and I need it now. This throbbing on my side is getting unbearable. I want my pain medication ASAP!"

"No."

"What do you mean . . . no?" I gasped.

"No as in no. We had a talk in Key West when we started to cut down on the medication. I told you then that you were going to have bad days, but you were going to have to tough it out unless you wanted to be addicted to this stuff the rest of your life."

"I'm not addicted!   How dare you?"

"Yes, you are and you will stay that way until we can safely reduce your dependence on pain medication.  Until then you are officially part of the Kentucky drug culture."

"But I'm in pain."

"I have no doubt that there is some residual pain, but it's bearable."

"How do you know it's bearable?  And why should I have to bear it?  Why should anyone have to be in any kind of pain if there is medication to eradicate it?"

"Because you'll be a slave to the medication otherwise."

"Bull.  The insurance companies don't want to pay for it, so they make this ridiculous policy that people should tolerate a standard level of pain.  I think that is crap and to make people needlessly suffer is evil."

"You don't have any health insurance.  If you stay like you are, you'll be an addict.  Case closed.  How are you going to pay for it all the time?  It's expensive."

"Are you for real, buddy?"  I could feel the blood run to my face and flung my words out with brutal carelessness.  "I fell forty feet off that fracking cliff and was only saved by slamming into a few trees on the way down.  My body basically broke into two parts.  I had to learn how to walk again and currently hobble to and fro with a limp and that's called progress.  I couldn't speak for months because my mouth was wired from the inside . . . and then my teeth had be pulled out in order to fix the rest of my pie hole. I have to wear this ridiculous hearing aid or learn sign language like Helen Keller. I pee on myself every time I burp. Now I have to endure being in pain because some penny-pincher bureaucrat in a tiny cubicle, who bangs the receptionist in the supply room but really gets his rocks off by telling people like me that the company has to make a profit, so for the stockholders' good I have to live with pain." Trembling with indignation, I gave a harsh derisive snort.

"Now I've been a good soldier. I have done everything asked of me. I've taken everything in stride. I know sometimes my manners are bad. I grieve over them on long winter nights, but for the most part, I did everything according to the medical scripture, endured every humiliating procedure and fought back the odds every day. I think even you would say that my recovery is near miraculous. So, is it too much to ask for a fresh pain patch or a shot when pain is the one thing I will not, should not and cannot endure?" Tears streamed down my face. "Damn you! I WANT MY PAIN MEDICATION!"

"What's going on here?" Matt asked in an uncertain tone. He entered the doorway, his patrician face lined with concern. "I could hear you both from outside."

Jake threw a glance at me. "I think you interrupted a hissy fit."

It was the first time I had seen Matt in six months. We talked several times on the phone each day, but I had kept him away. The truth was I didn't want him to witness my humiliating struggle to recover.

I recoiled as though Jake had slapped me. "A hissy fit? You refer to my suffering as a hissy fit, you condescending turd. If I were a man, you wouldn't dare treat me in this manner. Men always get more pain medication than women. Shame on you. Yes, shame on you, Jake Dosh."

Embarrassed that Matt was seeing me beg for drugs, I rushed to my bedroom, locking the door behind me. The rage I felt was pushed away in the desperate search for my private stash of ill-gotten pain pills that my daughter had stashed when inspecting the house last month. "Where did she put them?" I asked myself, tapping my forehead. My memory was not what it used to be. *Ahh. In my closet floor safe.* Dragging a chair over, I sat and leaned down trying to reach the floor dial. With hands trembling, I rotated the safe's dial. After many failed tries, I finally got the sequence right and yanked open the safe. Ensconced were small bags of potent painkillers and another one of weed. All illegal little goodies that my daughter had procured in case of a rainy day.

Well, it was pouring.

Each bottle and bag had written instructions but I was frantic, searching for something that would dull my horrible pain.

Ignoring Baby's scratching at the door, I happily swallowed a pill dry. Stumbling to my bed, I let my Egyptian cotton sheets enfold my aching body as I lit a pre-rolled joint and inhaled the gentle smoke, calming my boiling emotions and swirling mind. Taking only a couple of hits, I put the joint out. It was all I needed. Until my accident, I hadn't ever tried marijuana, but it helped with the nausea.

Rolling on my back, I thought about what Jake had said, but I wasn't sorry about my outburst. I wasn't sorry about my needing drugs. If high-powered painkillers were what it took for me to get through the day – so be it. After all, even Sherlock needed his seven-percent solution.

Folding my hurting limbs into the fetal position, I rocked myself, waiting for the pill to take effect until I heard a whimper and felt weight press on the mattress. It didn't occur to me how Baby got into the room as I reached over and patted his massive head. "Oh, Baby. Am I ever going to be well again? Is this the best it's going to get?" I whispered to the concerned mastiff.

Baby, with his large rough tongue, licked my arms as I rubbed his ears. When I stopped, he snorted in my face and circled three times before lying down in his bed. Listening to his contented breathing, I fell asleep. I dreamt that several honeybees flew into the room and crawled on my arm. I know their touch. One stung me. I must have rolled on her in my sleep. Or maybe she sacrificed herself for me so the cocktail of complex proteins in her venom would help ease my aching joints. Buzz. Buzz. Buzz. Zzzz.

# 7

Awakening to the pressure of someone scooting next to me in bed and then loudly crunching on cereal, I reached behind me and felt worn jeans covering skinny legs. "Morning, Franklin," I rasped.  My tongue was thick with a sticky film.

"Good morning, Miss Drama."  Crunch.  Crunch.

"Franklin, how did you get in my room?  Didn't I lock the door?"

"Not very effective if you leave the door to the patio open."

"I guess that would explain a cat sitting on my face," I replied, reaching up to unwrap a cat from around my head.  She purred at my touch.

"Ahh, don't.  She looks so comfy.  There's also another one curled up with Baby. You know, Sleeping Beauty you're not.  Besides a cat sitting on your head, your mouth was open, I guess so the earsplitting snoring could escape. The sound was vibrating off the walls."

"Well, you're no Prince Philip to wake up to," I replied, sitting up and throwing the cat to the floor. "Are there any other critters I need to be aware of?"

The cat stretched and jumped into a Hans Wegner Papa Bear chair. She was one of the barn cats who apparently had fled her rustic surroundings for a more luxurious lifestyle and had brought her boyfriend along. Rubbing my neck, I tried to get my bearings as I had been sleeping upside down on the bed.

"Haven't looked yet." Crunch. Crunch. Slurp.

"Is that a glass of milk?"

"Yep."

"Can I have a sip?"

"Why not. You paid for it." Franklin handed me a tall glass of milk, which I greedily drank.

"I guess you were sent in to determine if I was still in a horrible mood."

"Matt called me yesterday, very upset."

"Did he tell you I acted like a crazy person?"

"He said he wanted that glorious gray matter of yours sharp today. Very important, he said, so he sent me to get you ready." Franklin spooned in more cereal before he spoke. "Look, Josiah, there's no judgment here. Just concern about what is the best thing to do. We both feel that you saved our lives. I mean, you took that freak down. You took the fall, literally. And we are here to help – however long it takes, partly because we feel we owe it to you and partly 'cause we want to. We are both fond of you."

"Fond of me?"

"Okay, Matt loves you and I am very . . . fond of you . . . and frankly, life wouldn't sparkle as much without you. I want you to get very well."

"What's behind the kind words? I sense an unspoken agenda."

"Well, Miss Suspicious, if the truth must be told, Matt will not move forward emotionally or physically until things are settled with you, and by that, I mean you can function independently and the farm is shipshape. I can understand his feelings but frankly, my dear, I am a bit tired of it all. I want a life with Matt, but you are a buttinsky. As long as you are needy, Matt will be accommodating."

"Gee, Franklin. You make me feel all warm and cozy inside." I was very hurt by Franklin's words.

"Just letting you know where I stand. Personally, if you need drugs and dope to make you feel like a human being, I'll make sure you have drawers full of that stuff. Just let Matt go."

I tried not to show that Franklin was upsetting me. People were starting to make demands that I was not able to reciprocate yet. I was still a broken piece of china.

"Last night was the first time I had seen Matt in months. If you and Matt are having problems, I don't think it has anything to do with me," I said.

"Josiah, we never go anywhere. We never do anything except work on this stinking, rundown farm."

"Doesn't look rundown anymore."

"Yeah, thanks to Matt and me. Look at my hands. They are simply ruined."

"Franklin, when three people have had traumatic experiences like we did only a short time ago . . . it takes time to recover both physically and emotionally. Maybe you are rushing the healing process. Perhaps Matt is suffering from post-traumatic stress?"

"Let's not be overly dramatic. Just encourage Matt to get on with his own life. Okay?" Franklin pulled playfully at one of my toes. I winced.

"I will feel him out, but I can't promise anything. I just got home. I haven't even visited my bee yard yet."

"Well, Matt and Shaneika will be here at three o'clock. Apparently they want to talk with you about your lawsuit against the city. Matt wants you to have a clear mind, so take it easy on the pain killers today."

"I know this is hard for you to understand, but I am doing the best I can. A fifty-year-old asthmatic body doesn't heal as fast as a thirty-year-old one, but I'll think about what you said. Does everyone know about my private stash?"

"I put everything back – love the hidden safe, by the way – and told them you would be ready to do your therapy plus the meeting today."

"You're a good man, sister."

"Ahh, movie patter. You've been reading about the black bird lately."

"*The Maltese Falcon* was playing late last night. I got up at two and watched part of it."

Franklin did his Humphrey Bogart impersonation. "Listen. When a man's partner is killed, he's supposed to do something about it. It doesn't make any difference what you thought of him. He was your partner and you're supposed to do something about it."

I clapped my hands. "Can you do Sydney Greenstreet as the Fat Man?"

"No, but I can do a hell of a Peter Lorre. Did you know what Peter Lorre said to Vincent Price at Bela Lugosi's funeral?"

"Do you think we ought to drive a stake through his heart just in case?" I replied.

Franklin's face fell. "You always steal my thunder."

"Ask me something hard. Oh Franklin, don't be so childish. You seem to be angry that I actually lived through that night. Look at it this way. You are younger, healthier and stronger than I. You'll be living long after I'm dead. Now, doesn't that make you feel better?"

"Oddly, it does."

"Well, good. Now I feel like crap." Looking down, I was a wrinkled and stained mess. "I guess I need to apologize to Jake."

"What you need to do is do your therapy, get cleaned up, then have breakfast, which I will make for you. Look pretty for once." Franklin analyzed me. "Yes, a man might take your mind off your troubles," he mumbled.

"What's that?"

"Nothing, just thinking."

"Franklin, how about a quid pro quo? I will talk with Matt but . . ."

"Whaddja need?"

"Can you get on your computer and find out about the Silver Creek Vineyard and the Dunne family?"

"Like what?"

"Anything you can find out – bank records, lawsuits, just anything about Jamie Dunne's death. Pleeeease!"

"You got it." Franklin gave me a goofy smile. "Like old times. I just hope this doesn't end like our last investigation together."

"You and me both, sister. I'd like to get started on solid foods." I sat down on the bed. Suddenly, the thought of getting into my bathing suit just overwhelmed me. As if reading my thoughts, Franklin helped me to take off my dirty clothes and put on a muumuu. "While you are swimming, I will check your room for snakes."

"Oh goodness, please!"

"Shampoo and soap are by the outdoor shower. Now git, girl."

I limped out to the pool area looking for Jake. He was already in the water, which was steaming in the cool morning air.

"Come on in, Boss Lady; water's fine."

I carefully clung to the railing as I took one slippery step and then another until I was chest deep in the water. It did indeed feel warm and cozy.

Jake must have turned the heat up. He handed me water weights.

"Wait a minute, Jake," I said. "I need to talk with you."

He shook his head. "You don't need to say a thing. It was a bad day, that's all. Look, I have had tough battle-hardened s.o.b.s beg me to off them when they got hurt. They couldn't handle the pain. What your body was telling you was that we need to look at alternative ways to handle the pain, because you're getting used to the patch. I already have some ideas that we'll explore."

"What makes you think I was going to apologize?"

"Because," Jake grinned at me, "you like me. You really do."

"Jeez, you sound like Sally Field." I looked inquisitively at his ruddy face. "So – we're okay? No hard feelings?"

Jake palmed his thumb and pinky while holding up his hand. "Scout's honor."

"Were you a scout?"

"No, but I'm always prepared." He gave me a cheesy grin. "We're fine. I never take anything you say personally any-o-how. Now let's stop this touchy-feely stuff before I begin to cry. You cry enough for the both of us."

Jumping Jehosaphat, I thought, what a crummy morning. Feeling like a cranky old biddy, I did what I was told – for once.

# 8

Matt and Shaneika were seated very solemnly at my Nakashima table with their expensive briefcases open and files spilling out.

Shaneika put on her lavender reading glasses, which clashed with her short red dreadlocks. I guess the platinum crew cut wasn't working for her anymore.

Both were doing their best not to stare at me.

"Can I get you anything to drink?" I asked.

"No, thank you," answered Matt.

"No, thanks," murmured Shaneika, hiding behind some manila folders and glancing furtively in my direction.

"Okay, everyone put down the files and folders and take a good gander. Really, I mean it. I'm open for inspection."

Slowly two pairs of curious eyes, one a languid dark
blue, the other a bright hazel, slid up my torso and finally
rested on my face. Shaneika's eyes widened while Matt's
remained passive.

"It is what it is. What do you think?" I asked, keeping
my voice light.

"It's amazing," replied Shaneika. "When I saw you in
Key West, you were still pretty swollen and black-blue.
You look great. I mean, not just how they put you back
together but great, really good, pretty even. Matt, doesn't
she look awesome? Who would have thought after they
pulled you up from that ledge that they could have
repaired the damage to . . ."

"I don't want to talk about that night – ever. Josiah,
you look the same," Matt said.

"I do? I thought I look better, even younger.
Shaneika, don't you think I look younger?"

"Yes, now that you mention it, you do look younger."
Shaneika cocked her head in amazement. "I think you
look fantastic. You really got this Scandinavian look
going for you." She looked over at Matt. "You need to
quit being so traumatized, Matt. Josiah looks . . . "

"Put together?" I remarked.

Matt opened his notebook. "Let's move on to why
we're here. Shaneika, you start with the lawsuit and I'll
finish on the farm."

Shaneika shot Matt a protesting look and then raised
an eyebrow at me. "Okay. The city has offered us 1.2
million to be paid in four yearly payments."

"Anything else?"

"No."

"What are my medical bills up to now, including everything?"

"You're getting close to $900,000."

Jake, who was sitting behind me, let out a long low whistle.

"Does that include the doctors, house in Key West, the RV rental and Jake?"

"Everything up to two weeks ago. That's when I got the last invoices."

I swiveled toward Jake. "How many more months of recovery do I have?"

"For an accident like yours, I would say you've got another year to go. You will probably need some more minor surgery. After that, it's as good as it's going to get."

"Will I recover one hundred percent?"

Jake shook his head.

"What about the limp and the loss of hearing?"

"I'm not your primary doctor, but I would say these injuries are permanent."

"Might I have complications in the future?"

"Yes, but it is hard to predict which system might be affected first. Anything could blow up – stroke, renal failure. Your body could even reject the new hip prosthesis and phosphocalcic ceramic bone replacement. I know this sounds unpleasant, but it's the truth. But there is the other side – nothing could happen and you will live to a ripe old age."

Matt's face was turning a shade of olive green.

Shaneika leaned forward and stabbed a pencil in the air. "I know that Josiah is having problems with her pain management. Will her pain go away?"

"She will always have a level of pain to endure."

"Prescriptions?"

"She will be on pain medication of one sort or another until the day she dies according to the western idea of medicine."

"What else is there?"

"Well, I'd like to take her to an old-fashioned medicine man from my tribe. I think he could help her, or she could try acupuncture."

Shaneika started to speak.

I interrupted. "We'll talk about that later." I placed my hands on the table. "It looks like we are talking about an amount of money larger than 1.2 million dollars. That's just the current medical bills for now and not what I'll need in the future. What about my loss of income, damage to the house, Franklin's injuries and Baby's also?"

Matt cleared his throat. "Franklin has been compensated. His suit with the city is over." His blue eyes looked cloudy and dull. They would not remain on my face.

"What did he get?"

"I can't divulge that."

"Has Kelly been reimbursed for taking care of Baby?"

Shaneika spoke. "No. That is part of the settlement with the city. I didn't want to reimburse Kelly with the money I paid for the ten acres thinking that the city might dismiss the claim."

"What about all the repairs to the house?"

"Actually only a small amount of damage was done to the house by O'nan's attack. The bills for those repairs have been given to the city."

Matt interrupted. "The repairs for both the house and farm are in my report. Shaneika and I thought it best to pay for those separately according to the CPA's advice."

"I also included the costs for the security measures you installed when O'nan was hounding you," said Shaneika, "but I'm sure the city's attorney will try to get the judge to throw those out."

I thought for a moment. Not comprehending all the small details, I decided to concentrate on the big picture. "Shaneika, ask the city for twelve million to be paid in one lump sum."

"Josiah, be reasonable. Times are tough. The city doesn't have that kind of money and I'm not sure, even for your extensive injuries, that you are entitled to such a large amount."

"These are my instructions. Ask them for twelve million dollars or I am going to give an in-depth interview to the *Courier-Journal* about my experiences with the police department and how I almost got framed for murder when the death was eventually ruled accidental. I assume the mayor wants to run for governor in two years. The mayor's enemies will have a field day with it. Also I want some sort of health insurance the city will provide until Medicare kicks in."

Shaneika shook her head as she wrote on her legal pad. "You'll never get it."

"If they offer four million or above with health insurance included, take it. I want at least a million in one lump sum."

"But will you take $500,000 for a first payment?"

"Yeah, who wouldn't, but they don't need to know that. The health insurance is non-negotiable though. Really good health insurance would make me all giggly inside."

"Well, I think they were trying to bluff their way out, thinking you might be nervous and take anything they offered."

"Why would I do that? The worst is over. I survived the fall and have nothing but time to be a thorn in their side."

Shaneika gave Matt a sly glance, but he looked away. They said nothing but scratched on their legal pads.

There was something hanging in the silence that said – BEWARE! We sat for a moment as I looked into each of their faces. Behind me I heard Jake shift in his chair. Something of the Sherlock in me screamed – the game was afoot.

"What's the unspoken truth here? And don't say it is my imagination. One thing my accident has done is made me hypersensitive to my surroundings. Right now, both your auras are dancing around the rooms. What is it?"

"You were supposed to have been told in Key West," growled Matt, staring at Jake, "but the kid got called away on that Amsterdam case . . . and no one else had the nerve to tell you."

I think even then I knew what he was going to say, but I didn't want to hear it; yet I couldn't turn away. "You tell me, Matt." I could feel the hair on my arms begin to stand at attention.

"O'nan's body was never recovered. Neither the police nor your daughter's team could find him. In fact, the ferry was broken into that night. Its rowboat was stolen and was found across the river where a car was stolen from a driveway on down the road from there. He might have survived the fall. Being high, he may have been relaxed enough to have hit the water at the right angle . . ."

I swung around to Jake. "Is that why you were assigned to me . . . to take on O'nan if he showed up?"

"I was assigned to you because I've had special training in severe trauma like yours. You know that."

"What else did my daughter tell you to do?"

"I was to keep you from danger."

"Meaning?"

"I'm an expert in combat triage, small weaponry and martial arts. We figured if he came at you again, it would be at close range with a small pistol or knife . . . even his hands."

"You were the first line of defense. So if he got to me, you could patch me up long enough to get me to a hospital?"

"Something like that," agreed Jake. His eyes never wavered from mine.

"And Cody is the second?"

"He is the first line of defense. I'm backup."

"My life gets weirder and weirder. Why was my expensive electronic gate taken down?"

"Those things provide no real security for someone who really wants to get in. Besides, Matt said the gate would scratch the tour buses."

I started laughing. "God forbid we mar the paint on the tour buses." I rubbed my temples. I was getting a headache. I jerked my head up "Hey, what tour buses? What tour?"

"Yeah, yeah. I need to talk to you about that," said Matt giving Jake an annoyed look.

"Let's get back on track, guys. I'm sorry, Josiah," said Shaneika, "but this issue about O'nan was tough to call."

"No, I'm sorry. Sorry for all the unpleasantness I've brought into your lives. I'm sorry for the drama and the extra work; the fear I've brought into your existence. Shaneika, I haven't even visited your horse yet. And the thing is I don't know when things will get back to normal."

I leaned back in my chair. My left arm started to tremble. I placed my right hand on it, holding it down. "I knew. Deep down, I knew he might still be alive. No one mentioned the findings of his autopsy. I couldn't find anything about his funeral in the obits when I searched the computer. I knew. I just didn't want to face it."

Matt impatiently untied his tie and unbuttoned his collar. He took a deep breath. "I think I can speak for Shaneika too when I say that dealing with unfortunate circumstances is what we do. Without tragedy, we wouldn't have jobs."

"This is a little closer to home than I would like," interrupted Shaneika, "but I can handle it. After all, I have ancestors who were war heroes in every war since the Revolutionary War. They'd be ashamed if I couldn't handle one little white boy who acts like he's got no people."

I smiled at the southern expression for no 'counts. No one to teach him right from wrong. No one to stand up for him. No one to love him. That's what it means. A loner. Even though we Kentuckians have our share of kooks, a loner is still something to be mistrusted. People in Kentucky are family and clan-oriented.

We spent another half hour going over details before calling it quits. I was drained and so were Matt and Shaneika. Before she left though, I called Shaneika into my bedroom on the pretense of seeing my new Haitian paintings, which I had switched for the Bell landscapes. She loved them.

"Do I have any money left in my account from the Ellis Wilson painting?"

"Just about five thousand left. Everything has been spent on the lawsuit, of which I'm not taking a percentage; yes, thank you very much, Miss Shaneika."

"I do appreciate that you're not making money off my pain and suffering."

"Next time you sue someone, I won't be so generous."

"Still paying off that favor you owe my daughter, huh?"

My fussy lawyer pretended she didn't hear me.

"I would love to know what she's got on you. Enough of that. Shaneika, do you know that Irene Meckler came to visit me in Key West?"

"Yes."

"Did you know that her nephew drowned last month?" I gave her an exaggerated, sad face. "She's asked me to look into it. The boy was only fifteen. A baby."

Shaneika took a pen from her breast pocket and began writing on her arm. "Good golly almighty! What do you want?"

"A look at the police and coroner's reports. Also any insurance reports. Things like that."

"Oh, you mean easy things to get," she sputtered sarcastically.

"I'm sure you have contacts in Jessamine County."

"I'll see what I can do." She pointed a finger at me. "No promises though. I'll call tomorrow and get the details from you."

"I just happened to have made a list of his name, address, Social Security number, school, you know, stuff like that," I said, pulling a paper out from my cleavage. The paper was warm.

"Can you please not store documents between your bosoms? It's a filthy habit." She held the paper by her fingertips and sniffed it. "At least it smells like Chanel No. 5 . . . and mint?"

"Vicks VaporRub."

"Of course, Vicks always goes well with a French perfume." Shaneika made for the door. "I'm going to see *my* baby, give him a good rubdown, feed him some grain and then flee back to the city where things are normal." Her heels made a clicking noise down the tiled hallway.

"Call me when you've got something," I called after her.

"Like I got time to snoop around about a dead boy," I heard her grouse under her breath.

Alone now, I looked around the room. Feeling uneasy, I checked the closet area, looked behind the door in the bathroom, opened the patio door and called for Baby, locked same door once he was inside, closed the drapes, locked the steel bedroom door, caressed the panic button installed by my bed, made sure the baby monitor was on and repositioned the stun gun under my pillow.

Matt softly knocked on my door. "Babe, we need to talk about the farm," he said in his low husky voice, which used to thrill me.

"Later, Matt. I'm drained. Gonna take a nap."

"Okay. What about dinner?"

"Not hungry. Just need some time by myself."

After hearing Matt reluctantly plod away, I got out a little tub of ice cream from my miniature freezer, and sitting on the bed with my trusty legal pad, began making notes about Jamie Dunne. I needed something constructive to take my mind off my own problems, and to do something positive for someone else. Like most independent people, I felt guilty about relying on other people, but I had no choice at the moment. I could only do what I could. But I could help put Sarah Dunne's mind at ease about her baby boy. Yes, that I could do.

*

At eleven that night the phone woke me up. I had fallen asleep on a pile of yellow sheets of paper.

"Hello?" I answered groggily.

"I'm sorry about O'nan," said the voice on the other end of the phone.

"Don't worry about it. It's out of your hands."

"We looked for him everywhere. I still have operatives trying to track him down."

"He may be really dead. We have no real proof he is alive. Don't spend any more money on me. Come back home."

"I . . . I'll be home soon. I'm almost finished here. Then we can work on a plan to flush out O'nan if he's around."

"We're going to do no such thing. We are going to get back to normal, as much as we can. He's dead."

"That is not a wise plan of action."

"Just come home. We'll argue about this later. Oh, by the way, did you recover the stolen painting?"

"Yes, I got it."

"Want to tell your old mother which painting it was?"

"Can't."

"Bad guys in jail?"

"Some are."

"And the rest?"

Silence hovered, then a click. "Talk to you later." The call was over.

I did not feel reassured. Not one little bit.

# 9

Dressed, teeth brushed, hair combed, makeup on, I strode – well, limped – with purpose into the great room the next morning. No one was about, but I heard noise from the patio. There I found Matt shoving a cheese Danish in his mouth while trying to read the paper.

"Morning," he said apprehensively.

"Good morning," I answered with a bright smile. "Shouldn't you be at work?"

"Well, I am working although it's Saturday."

"Seem to have lost track of the days," I mused over juice. "Where's Jake?"

"Jake has the day off and has gone to Hopkinsville to see the Trail of Tears memorial. Cody is hanging around somewhere. I thought I'd take you around the farm and show you the improvements, talk about your finances, that is, if you are up to it."

"I am, but I warn you that I tire easily and might have to take breaks."

"No problem. How about some pastries and then we'll get going?"

"Sounds good," I replied before sipping on orange juice. "I'm in your capable hands."

Matt nodded, but I am sure he felt the way I did. The old intimacy was gone and though we were polite with one another, our being together felt strained.

I ate a strawberry pastry very slowly and drank a large glass of milk. Chewing still irritated my tender mouth, but I couldn't eat baby food forever.

Once done, Matt and I got in the second-hand electric golf cart my daughter had purchased for me so I could get around the farm. The morning promised a sunny spring day as chattering songbirds were busily gathering materials for their nests. The viburnum bushes were perfuming the air with their white blossoms. It was great to be outside and the cart drove smoothly to the beginning of the property.

During the drive, Matt wove a story of repairs that included a new gravel road, mowed fields that had been resown with Dutch white clover seed, orchard trees pruned, dead trees removed and new fruit trees planted. Blackberry and raspberry bushes planted on the road side of pasture fences; the house power-washed, refurbished, new toilets, sinks and solar water heaters installed; chipped tile and slate floors repaired; the pool fixed, the old cabana torn down; and all the work sheds and outbuildings repaired and painted.

Matt brought the cart to a halt in the bee field. All the hives had a fresh coat of paint and the honey supers were sitting high on the hive bodies. The field was alive with spring flowers like henbit and snowdrops while the honeysuckle hedges were beginning to open their flower buds. Dozens of bees swirled around the cart, curious. Several hovered around my face and then darted off. It was nice to drink in the scent of bee again.

"Well, what do you think?"

"Matt, everything looks fantastic. The woods have been kept intact while the pastures are clean. It looks like a real working farm. You did a great job." I looked about with pride. "But I'm just worrying – how much did this all cost?"

"Shaneika paid for the fences and the remodeling of the barn as she promised. The other repairs cost close to $300,000."

"Ouch. So that's where my Henry Faulkners went." I was quiet for a moment. "So Shaneika's $200,000 is . . ."

"Gone," stated Matt. "You have your retirement fund intact and your emergency $16,000. Everything else went back into the farm, but you are debt free."

"Except for the medical bills, which are going to be out of this world," I sighed.

"The farm was falling apart. Your daughter didn't know if you would be able to come back, so her decision was based on the need to sell. In the beginning, the doctors were not hopeful . . ." He stopped and stared.

It was a moment or two before he collected himself. "This way you will be able to get top dollar if you decide to pull out."

"I'm not criticizing, Matt. The place looks wonderful. I know it was touch and go there for a while." I squeezed his hand. "I know how far I've come and I know how far I've yet to go. No, this is going to be a long process. It's just that . . . how am I going to have money to live on – to pay the butcher, the baker, the candlestick maker?"

"I have a plan."

"You do?" I asked hopefully.

"*Architectural Digest* did not cancel. They came and photographed while you were in Key West. I gave them some old pictures of you and Brannon that will accompany the piece also announcing that the Butterfly is open for tours."

I started to object. I didn't like the idea of strangers gawking at my personal things.

"Now hear me out first. The tours are open only two days a week. Once visitors are done here, they visit Lady Elsmere's farm where she has built a gift shop to part them from their hard-earned cash. They can buy all sorts of trinkets with pictures of the Butterfly and Brannon's other successes imprinted. Lady Elsmere is going to split the proceeds with you fifty-fifty after expenses and also Charles' daughters will be the tour guides. You don't have to lift a finger. Cody has also worked out the security problems with them, so we don't need worry about that angle."

"Does June need money?"

"She's rich as Midas. Lady Elsmere is doing this for enjoyment as well as a tax write-off. She thinks you plunging off that cliff was the most exciting thing that has happened for a long time and she is going to make a killing off it – no pun intended."

"Jeeez. Sounds like that old bat."

"Number two. You are going raise the price of your honey. Everyone will buy because they'll be coming to take a gander at you. They will be willing to pay the honey price. I calculate that you might make $10,000 more this year from honey sales.

"Number three. Shaneika arranged for some of her buddies to board their horses here. You've got plenty of room and Charles' grandsons have agreed to take care of the horses.

"Number four. I'm going to start paying rent on the cottage."

"No, you're not. I'm going to put my foot down on that. Absolutely not. I mean it, Matt. Who paid for the materials to fix that pig's shed?"

Matt remained silent.

"I thought so. Gather all the receipts and when I get money from the city, I'll settle up with you. You're not going to pay for fixing up that broken-down excuse of a cottage. Besides, I don't think you'll be here for much longer if Franklin has his way."

"Is he on that rag again?" A bee settled on Matt's face. He wiped it impatiently away.

"Let's move the cart. You've set off her attack pheromones." Once a bee is hit, she releases chemicals that tell other bees she has been attacked and they come to help her.

Matt maneuvered the cart while raving. "Franklin wants to live in the city. He likes to eat out every night. I don't. By the time work is finished, I'm sick of Lexington. The drive to the farm relaxes me, and just being where there is no noise is calming. I'm not ready to settle down. I want to give my career at least two more years before taking the plunge, but Franklin will not quit pestering me."

"He wants to nest," I commented.

"To tell you the truth, I'm still getting over that awful night. I was parking the van when I heard your scream and the gunshots. I caught sight of O'nan through the window. Everything happened so fast. I called the police. Then another shot. I ran around to side of the house and cut off the power. I was going to enter by one of the back entrances but as I turned the corner, I saw you and O'nan go over the side. My God, the screaming was horrible. I heard you crash into every tree until that awful thud . . . and then nothing."

Matt became more agitated. "I didn't know what to do. I tried to climb down, but it was too steep and dark. I thought you were dead. I ran back into the house to search for Franklin. He had opened the front door somehow and was crawling down the driveway. I stopped the bleeding and carried him back into the house. By that time the police had arrived. I turned the electricity back on so those guys could see to climb down the cliff." Matt closed his eyes. "I just get the shakes thinking about it. Everything was in slow motion for me, but they had you stabilized in an hour. It took them two hours to get you up the cliff, though. The thing that is so ironic about this affair is that Franklin remembers nothing and you remember everything until the fall."

"Franklin has no memory?"

"None. Except for an occasional shoulder twinge, Franklin has totally recovered both mentally and physically. In fact, he's better because he loves all the attention. The story he tells is what he has read in the paper. Franklin is living in tall cotton and I'm struggling . . . to put the pieces back together."

"Franklin thinks that you feel guilty."

"I'm still recovering for sure. I have a list of things that need to be accomplished and I can't think of moving forward until then. I should have walked in the house with you. With three of us, Franklin and I could have taken him down."

"Nobody could have changed the outcome. If you had been in the house, I am sure he would have killed you first because you are the strongest of the three of us. O'nan was crazy that night. He was high on something. The fact you turned off the lights probably saved my life. If I hadn't been so fat, Matt, I could have run faster. He just caught me, that's all." I looked out, watching the orderly lives of the honeybees. "Mark me off your list, Matt. I'm not your responsibility. The farm and the Butterfly are in terrific shape. There won't be any problem if I'm forced to sell. She'll go fast. I'm ahead of Jake's recovery schedule, although he warned me that I might hit a plateau in that area, but that is in God's hands, not yours. You've done all that you can do for me. You're free. Be happy."

"Are you happy?"

"The way I look at it, every day is a gift. Just to see the Butterfly the way she is now is more than I had hoped for."

Matt kissed my cheek. I laid my head on his shoulder as we sat in silence watching the bees collect nectar from flowers and hurry back to the hives. I was happy as I had my Matt back.

We both were luxuriating in the quiet until a murder of crows put up a ruckus as a sparrow hawk glided past. Matt started the golf cart and said suddenly, "If Franklin doesn't get off my back, I may have to cut him loose."

I didn't answer, but thought that would be a mistake. Franklin was good for Matt as he tended to brood too much. Franklin was light where Matt was dark, both physically and emotionally. They complemented each other. For some reason Matt was angry with Franklin. I would have to find out why.

Matt let me off at the front door to the Butterfly, telling me that he would be at home if I needed him. I passed through the alcove gate and met Cody waiting for me with his hand on his gun.

"I would appreciate it if you'd let me know if you are leaving the house," said Cody, looking down at me.

I had a sudden impulse to squeeze his biceps. They looked like porch columns. "Sorry," I said, seemingly contrite, but not really sorry at all. "You up to a little wine tasting?"

Cody scowled.

"I want you to drive me over to Old Spears Vineyard. It's only ten minutes from here."

"What for?"

"A little intelligence gathering. I'll buy you lunch," I said, hoping to sweeten the pot.

"You got a deal, lady, but no alcohol for you – Jake's orders."

Within a half hour, I was ordering lunch on Old Spears' deck, as the day was warm. The waiter told me that they were not usually open for lunch, but Maggie Moore, the owner, had told them to open the kitchen when I called and told her that I was coming over. I sighed with contentment. I loved special treatment.

We were just getting our salads when Maggie walked in. Like Sarah Dunne, Maggie was petite but with shoulder-length chestnut hair and an infectious laugh. Old Spears Vineyard was known for its French night dinners of eight courses for which Maggie had traveled to France to learn to cook. Sitting down at the table, she motioned for the waiter to bring us a bottle of wine. Cody picked up his plate and moved to another table where he could witness all the entrances to the deck.

Maggie gave him an appraising look. "Goodness, what a bootie on that guy. I bet you could bounce quarters off it." She giggled. The waiter handed her a glass of red

wine. "Our First Spears Reserve made from
Chambourcin, Norton and Cabernet franc grapes. Here's
to your continued health, Josiah – the woman with nine
lives. Salut." She took a sip. "So you're back." She
looked hard at me. "What's that thing?" she asked,
pulling on my hearing aid.

"What does it look like? Hey, give it back."

She held the aid up to the sun inspecting it. "It looks
like something a spy would wear. Very sexy."

"That's what I think every morning when I put it on –
my *sexy* hearing aid. It beats a thong hands-down." I
grabbed it from her hand and put it back on.

"And you've lost a lot of weight. You look good." She
leaned forward and peered into my face. "Very good.
That black cane gives you the right air of mystery, but I'm
not going to give you any more compliments. I'm so
mad at you. You never returned one of my emails."

"That's one of the reasons I'm here, Maggie: to
apologize in person. I'm so sorry, but I was doped up for
the first several months and exhausted during the others.
I did appreciate the funny cards you sent. It was a boost
to my poor spirits."

Maggie pouted. "Well, at least you got them. Matt
promised me that you would, but . . ."

"I know. I know. I'm truly sorry. I should have made
more of an effort to let you know what was going on
with me."

She sipped her wine as the waiter brought me some iced tea. "What is the other thing that brought you here?"

"What?" I answered distractedly while slurping my tomato bisque. It was really good, thick and creamy.

"You said one of the reasons you came."

"Do you know Sarah Dunne?"

"Very well. Why?"

"Irene Meckler, my friend, is sister to Sarah and wants me to look into the death of her nephew, Jamie."

Maggie paused before placing her glass on the table. Her perkiness disappeared as a thoughtful expression froze into a frown. "Poor Sarah. Things have been rough for her. Her husband died several years ago from cancer and now her youngest child from a freak accident. Some people have rotten luck."

"Have you heard any rumors about her – something hinky?"

"Sarah's a good person. Her husband's death was hard on her, but with the insurance money, she was able to put some away for a rainy day. The business is not going as well as it should, but it still pays the bills. I talked with her at a conference earlier this year, and she was very hopeful that this season would be better."

"Was she dipping into her savings?"

"No, she was solvent. And Jamie was with her. He seemed very devoted to his mother."

"Did she complain about anything?"

"Just the usual complaints all business people have – high taxes, crazy customers, staff not showing up for work – things like that."

"Did you know anything about Jamie? Like – did he have a girlfriend? Did he have trouble at school? Sarah say anything about that?"

Maggie shook her head. "No. As far as I know, Jamie was a decent sort of fellow. No problems. His death was a shock to everyone." She waved to some customers leaving with shopping bags loaded with Old Spears Vineyard's wine. "Aren't you going to eat anything else besides soup?"

I grinned. "I wouldn't turn down any of your chocolate mousse cake."

"You're like an old person gumming soft foods."

I tapped my teeth with my fingernail. "Still getting used to the new choppers."

Maggie motioned for Cody to rejoin me. "I have to get back to work, but I will send out some cake. Hey, where did you get the new boyfriend? Isn't he too much car for you?"

"Thanks for the confidence booster, but I'm not driving him. He's not my boyfriend."

"Then what is he?"

"My bodyguard."

"Why can't you ever give a simple answer to a simple question? I swear, Josiah, bodyguard, indeed."

I shrugged.

Maggie gave Cody a big smile before she left. He sat down at my table again with a large plate of roasted duck. The waiter brought over more bread.

"This is my second plate," he announced with relish.

"You should come during a French night meal. Eight courses."

"Really?"

"I'll make arrangements for you. In fact, I think all of us could use a pleasant break."

Maggie brought out some hot chocolate mousse cake. I noticed that she had given Cody twice the usual serving. Someone had a crush. She mouthed, "he's cute" to me. I waved her away, chortling.

When finished, I made a reservation for the next French dinner. I also bought some of their award-winning wine plus some honey mead, which Maggie made from my honey. The clerk refused my money. "Everything's on the house today," she said, handing me back my debit card.

"That's cool," said Cody.

I was so touched I couldn't respond. I just nodded, making a mental note to treat Maggie better in the future. No more telling her customers that I had found a hair in her food. Maggie never did enjoy my sense of humor, but then she shouldn't have told folks that my honey was nothing more than bee vomit.

When I got back home, I wrote on my legal pad – interview with Maggie – bust! I had learned nothing useful.

# 10

The next several weeks were routine, routine, routine. Cody made his rounds of the farm like a little wind-up soldier, and Jake was constantly pushing me physically when not taking me to doctors' appointments, which were becoming fewer in number. There was some talk about another bone graft, but that died down after some tests.

Matt finished the caretaker's house and invited me to dinner. Small but cozy, just perfect for a single person, the sparsely furnished four rooms with colors of pale greens and browns reflected Matt's aesthetic taste. After the main course, we sat on the little porch and watched my peacocks strut in the yard while the sun settled in the distance behind the Berea knobs, the last gasp of the Appalachian Mountains before they gave way to the graceful hills of the Bluegrass. From Matt's porch, one could see for fifty miles or more.

To the south of Matt's porch vista was Whitehall, the home of Cassius M. Clay, the fiery emancipationist, who donated land for Berea College where beginning in 1855, both blacks and whites could get an education. This was stopped by the Day Law in 1904, when a member from the Kentucky legislature attended a graduation ceremony. Appalled at seeing integration, he drummed Jim Crow through the legislature at the next session. Black Kentuckians couldn't get an education at schools where whites attended until the law was amended again in 1950. This story was not one of Kentucky's finest.

But every time I saw the knobs, I thought of Berea College's creed – "God has made of one blood all peoples of the earth."

Awakening from his nap and not finding me home, Baby followed my scent to the cottage. Feeling threatened upon seeing him, the male peacock gave a grand display of his turquoise feathers while hissing at Baby, who took no notice of him. Giving me an accusing look, the fawn mastiff plopped down near the porch steps and would not be comforted until Matt had given him a plate of leftovers.

"I think I better be going," I replied to Matt's inquiry about dessert.

"I'll drive you home."

"I'll walk. Can still see. It's just turning dusk."

Matt looked dubious but said, "Call me when you reach the Butterfly so I won't worry. I'll call Jake and tell him you are on your way."

"Sure thing." I grabbed my cane and after waving goodbye, started down the gravel driveway to my house. The gravel was tedious to walk on, but I was too proud to say that I had made mistake and needed a ride home. Matt watched me for a moment and then went into the house. Baby, realizing that he might have to sleep outside if he didn't come with me, lumbered to his feet and followed at a distance. I pulled a taser out of my pocket in case a coyote got too inquisitive. Just the noise of a taser would make a coyote think twice.

Seeing that the lights were on in the old tobacco barn, I went in and found Shaneika brushing her stallion, who stirred at my entrance. "Whoa boy, whoa. She's not going to hurt you," soothed Shaneika. She rubbed his velvety muzzle, giving the horse a peppermint.

I stayed a safe distance away, plopping down on a bale of hay. "You really went and bought a racehorse. He's so beautiful," I said, admiring the horse's gleaming dark coat and black mane. "What's his name?"

"Comanche," she said, brushing his mane while the stallion chewed contentedly. "I felt he needed a strong name. Not after the tribe, but a documented survivor of Custer's stand at Little Big Horn."

"I knew that," I relayed, batting my eyelashes. I guess the name referred to a horse since no white soldier at the battle survived that day. I would have to look it up when I got home. "I would have just called him Scout."

"As in Tonto's horse?"

"Hey, you know your horses."

"You're not the only one who has useless information rolling around in her head. You renamed those nags you saved Scout and Silver. It doesn't take much to realize you have a thing for the Lone Ranger."

"Everyone should know things like that. It is part of our cultural history. What was the name of Dale Evans' horse?"

"Buttermilk."

"How about Gene Autry's horse?"

"Champion."

"Okay. How about the horse from Mister Ed?"

Shaneika gave me a weird look. "Uh, Mister Ed."

"Oh yeah, right. Well, the Lone Ranger is a cherished icon from my childhood. I wish I had kept my Lone Ranger lunchbox. It would be worth a small fortune now."

"Have you read that material I sent you?" asked Shaneika, wishing to change the subject.

"Not yet. I need to do that soon, as Irene will be asking for answers." I summed up my meetings with Sarah Dunne and Maggie Moore. Franklin had also sent me information, which I hadn't studied yet. It was just depressing, sifting through a dead boy's life. "What do you think?" I asked.

"I think Jamie was no different from any other boy of fifteen. He had secrets from his family. From what you told me, it seems he was sexually active."

"Yeah, but with whom? Everyone I've talked to confirms that he went to school and came straight home afterwards. When he wasn't working on the farm, he was on the river."

"Didn't you say that a girl his age worked at the vineyard?"

"She said there wasn't anything between them."

"And you believed her?"

"Maybe I should talk to her again. You're right. If I were she, I wouldn't tell something like that to a stranger." Seeing that it was now the last gasp of twilight, I hummed the *William Tell Overture* as I waved. "Farewell, Kemosahbee!"

Heading home, Baby rejoined me from a foray into the woods. I sang *Happy Trails* to him until I came to the bee yard. "Just gonna take a quick look-see," I said to Baby. Turning into the bee pasture, I was about eight feet in when I spied a dark figure moving near my hives.

I gasped. I couldn't get out any more sounds. Sensing my fear, Baby purposely moved in front of me, pressing against my legs, growling. Upon hearing the dog's warning, the shadowy figure looked up, only to flee into the woods. I grabbed Baby's collar and pulled him with me as I hobbled down the gravel road. Wanting to protect me, Baby jerked loose and ran in circles, only impeding my way. "Don't make me fall, Baby. I won't be able to get back up," I cried at the frantic dog. Finally remembering the emergency necklace that Jake had given me, I pushed on the panic button, again and again.

It must have been just over three minutes, when a jeep with bright search lights came rushing up the road. I pounded on the car hood as Jake and Cody jumped out of the jeep. Jake pushed me into the vehicle as Cody searched the perimeter with his gun drawn. Jake yelled at me to get down while he swerved the jeep around and headed toward the house. Cody jumped on the running board and held on. Once home, they surrounded me until they got me into the Butterfly. The phone was ringing. Jake answered it and muttered something like . . . "hurry!" It must have been either Shaneika or Matt calling.

Cody brought me a glass of water and then left to search the property. Jake ran to get the nebulizer as I had begun a serious asthma attack. I slid to the floor as Matt suddenly appeared before me in a T-shirt and boxer shorts. He lifted me into a chair.

Out of the corner of my eye, Brannon was sitting in his favorite chair reading the newspaper. "Now?" he mouthed to me.

*Go away, Brannon*, I thought. Looking disappointed, Brannon shimmered and then was gone.

I had more pressing problems than a dead husband beckoning from beyond the grave. It felt like someone was standing on my chest. Heaving for air, I tore at my shirt.

Matt grabbed my hands as he yelled at Jake to hurry. Everything seemed on the verge of going dark when Jake rushed into the room and threw Matt an adrenaline pen before he plugged in the nebulizer and poured abuterol into its opening. Matt tore off the cap of the pen and plunged the needle into my thigh.

I jerked forward.

Seconds later a life-saving steam emerged from the nebulizer mouthpiece, which Jake pushed into my mouth. The medicine found its way into my lungs, allowing my chest to expand more until my inhaling was longer and smoother.

Matt let go of my hands.

Opening my eyes, I saw Shaneika standing tightly in a corner. She looked frightened. Jake spoke with her before she gave me one last quick look and departed.

Finally my breathing was slow and steady.

Jake turned off the machine and removed its mouthpiece.

I was terrified. The idea that O'nan might be on the property was causing me to spin out of control just when I needed to focus. Plus my chest and thigh hurt like the dickens. Blood dripped from my cheek where I had scratched myself.

"Why did you push the panic button?" questioned Jake, speaking very loudly.

"Someone in the bee yard. When he heard me, he ran. It's O'nan. I think he's here!" I cried out. I tried to get up but Jake pushed me back into the chair.

He said something else to me.

"What? What are you saying? Can't hear you. Speak up."

Cody strode in with my hearing aid and a carved piece of wood. He shook his head at Jake as he dropped the hearing aid in my lap.

Jake checked it and put it on my ear as my hands were shaking far too violently to help. "Can you hear more clearly?" asked Jake.

I nodded. Cody handed me the carved wooden stick. "What's this?" I asked.

Jake gave a slight nod of his head, giving Cody to signal to depart, which he swiftly did. Pulling up a chair, Jake sat down. His forehead was deeply creased and his jowls seemed slack as though his skin had been pulled loose. "Man, I feel really bad about this. I should have warned you," he confessed.

"That O'nan is in Lexington?" I couldn't stop shivering.

"Boss Lady, it's not O'nan. It's not someone who will hurt you." Jake looked helplessly at Matt. "I don't know how to explain this. We thought it best not to tell you because we never thought you would see him."

Matt leaned forward and held my hand. "It's not O'nan. It's Boo Radley."

"Huh? Talk sense, Matt," I demanded.

"It's not the Boo Radley; it's *your* Boo Radley. That's the best way to explain it."

"Like Boo Radley from *To Kill A Mockingbird*?"

"When the rescue team brought you up, you had a tree branch through your thigh. One of the paramedics pulled me aside and told me what a good job I had done; otherwise you would have bled out. He then asked me how I could have gotten down and back up the cliff so fast.

"Like I told you before. I didn't go down the cliff. I couldn't see in the dark. I thought you were dead. I went to find Franklin. But when the paramedics got to you, the branch had been trimmed with a knife and a tourniquet was tied on your leg, plus there was moss packed around the branch to stanch the bleeding. Whoever it was knew enough not to pull the branch out of your leg."

I listened, but could barely believe what I was hearing.

Matt continued his monologue as though reliving a dream. "When the big kahuna arrived the next afternoon, I told her about the tourniquet. Her first thought was it might have been O'nan, but she ruled out that possibility two days later when her men discovered a cave in the Palisades cliffs about three miles from here."

"What did she find?" I asked, my heart pumping fast.

To my chagrin, Matt's lips turned into a short smile.

"This is not funny," I fumed.

"Actually, it is. Our mistake was not telling you about it, but we thought you would never see him." Matt took a deep breath. "She found a hermit who had been living in a cave for over a year without detection."

"A hermit! Is he crazy?"

"Nope. His background is good. No history of drugs, violence or anti-social behavior. The situation was explained to him. He was very cooperative and let us check him out. He turns out to be a true ascetic. Wants only to be left alone so he can contemplate God. Came here because he said Kentucky was a very spiritual place. He's actually a very nice guy. But what makes him so odd is that he's an ex-rapper Hasidic Jew from the East Coast. Since we knew your beliefs of live and let live, she didn't run him off. He wasn't living on your property anyway and had saved your life."

I squinted at Jake and Matt. Would they lie to me about O'nan only to replace it with a more outrageous lie? What was the truth here?

"What's his name?"

"His real name is Moshe Goren, but his stage name is Magnus J."

I studied the wood. It was a handsomely carved walking stick with figures of honeybees and occult signs. "These are kabbalah symbols," I said, turning the wood over.

"How can you tell?" asked Jake.

"Because I was once a professor of art history specializing in religious symbols," I quipped. I pointed to a symbol. "This is the kabbalah tree of life. This sign over here is the circle of the five worlds. Each ring in the circle represents a plane of existence – God, emanation, creation, formation and action. This group of symbols with the Hebrew letters and the eye represents protection against the evil eye."

"It must be a gift for you, Josiah," said Matt, fingering the carving of a queen bee. "He's leaving gifts for you like Boo Radley did for Jean Louis and Jem."

"That's great. Just great. I've always said what I need is an ex-rapper Hasidic Jew carving mystical prayer canes for me, sneaking around on my property like some nut and scaring the bejeebies out of me. Now I can see why you didn't think you needed to tell me about him."

I was so mad I could have spit cotton. I grabbed my walking stick and hobbled into the kitchen, where I got a gallon of vanilla ice cream plus a spoon and marched past Jake to my office. "Don't say a thing to me," I muttered. "I'm going to eat every bit." I slammed the office door and sat on the corner of my desk eating ice cream.

Suddenly feeling nauseous, I put the container outside the door and let Baby finish the rest of it at his post of guarding the hallway.

He put the tub between his two mammoth paws and buried his face in the container happily.

I picked up the wooden walking staff and examined it. It was made of sycamore wood, probably found floating in the river. It was not professionally carved, nor sandpapered or even stained. It was a rough piece of wood, but it had a powerful quality about it. Obviously someone had taken much time to carve all the symbols and flying honeybees. It was folk art in its most primitive and raw form.

I felt drawn to it.

Walking around the room, it felt natural to be by my side as though it had be specially designed for me. I decided it would be my country walking staff and the cane Franklin got me would be my town cane.

I tossed the staff in the corner. My throat felt raw and my ribs were throbbing. I took a hit of the abuterol spray kept on the desk. My body was literally quivering from all the adrenaline. Be careful, I thought, adrenaline is what did Richard Pidgeon in. Ignoring the shaking, I booted up my computer. While waiting for my tired old machine to respond, I opened the mail. Bills, bills and more bills.

I came across Shaneika's folder and tentatively opened it. As I had hoped, it contained copies of Jamie Dunne's coroner's report and death certificate. It was sad reading. Jamie's body contained no drugs, no sign of disease; just a healthy Kentucky boy on his way to manhood. His face, arms and hands contained scratches that were indicative of someone tipping over in a kayak and struggling near the bank where there were sharp rocks. There was one contusion on the left side of his head that could have been caused by him rushing up from the water and hitting his head on the overturned kayak. No suspicion of foul play. Death was ruled accidental. I put the documents in a file marked Jamie and put it aside.

Under various clothing catalogs was an envelope from Franklin. The word PRIVATE was scratched on it along with a frowning smiley face. *Not good.*

I tore it open.

Franklin had gone on Facebook and MySpace to track down Jamie's friends who were on Sarah's list. He had downloaded pages with photos of Jamie with his friends at school functions. A blond-haired Jamie with his tanned muscular arms around several girls at a dance. Jamie with his buddies giving wannabe gang symbols. Jamie and others skateboarding in the school parking lot. Jamie and another boy leaning against an old ratty car smiling innocently at the photo taker. There was no patter by his friends thinking his death was anything but an accident. This was a big help. The last thing I wanted to do was to interview his friends and have a slew of angry parents on my fanny.

The last page was a picture downloaded from YouTube of a group of army nurses in the desert singing *Girls Just Wanna Have Fun*.

Franklin had circled something behind them, but I couldn't make out what it was. Pulling out my magnifying glass, I studied the photo under a light, but my hands were still trembling so much, I couldn't make out what he wanted me to see.

My computer beeped in readiness. I typed in YouTube and then the name of the video Franklin had written for me in bold letters.

Five army nurses in desert fatigues with arms locked around each other giggled to Cyndi Lauper's song while kicking up their legs. Behind them, trucks and personnel scooted back and forth whipping up dust. They must have been in front of a heavily traveled road.

A jeep stopped with several official-looking men as a woman dressed in black walked from the left side of the frame and stood next to the jeep conversing. She was wearing Kevlar and lugging a huge official-looking briefcase handcuffed to her wrist. A man scooted over to make room for her in the jeep. She turned for an instant and gave the briefest frown at the singing nurses before turning back to the men in the jeep. She said something to the men.

The driver of the jeep yelled at the nurses and one woman went to turn the video off. Then the video ended.

NO! IT COULDN'T BE!

I brought the video up again and again. I couldn't testify positively in a court of law, but in my heart I knew. I picked up the phone and put it down. Jake had probably already made his call. All I had to do was wait.

At ten, the phone rang. I called out from my bed that I had it. "Hello."

"Hey. Heard you had a bad asthma attack. How are you doing?"

"Better. But, of course, if I had been told of a hermit lurking about the property, I might have been better prepared."

"That was my call. Now I realize that it was a stupid one, but you had so much on your plate. I thought if you hadn't detected him in a year, you still wouldn't see him for another one. I'm sorry. It was a bad decision."

"Yes, it was. You are distracted and not realizing that these little surprises are taking a toll on me."

Her response was silence.

"Well, it's over now. There's no use in talking about it. I'm fine. Just shaken up a little bit," I said, softening.

"I feel so bad about it."

"How's Amsterdam?" I interrupted. "Case almost finished?"

"Yes, but then I have to go to London for several weeks. After that I should be home."

"How's the weather in Amsterdam?"

"Uh, cold and wet."

"Not hot and dry like a sandy desert in Afghanistan!" Pause. "I'm in Amsterdam."

"You're lying. You told me that you wouldn't take a military contract. You promised." I swear her breathing stopped for several seconds.

"Things changed after your accident. Hard decisions had to be made and I made them."

"What good is my recovery if you're dead? What is the point of my living if you're gone? No, this will not do."

"We will discuss it when I get home."

"No," I said. "We will discuss it now. I'll sell the Butterfly before I let you risk your life to pay my medical bills."

There was a click and the phone went dead.

"Don't you dare hang up on me!" I yelled. "Hello. Hello. Are you there?" The line was silent. "Jumping Jehosaphat!" I shouted as I crashed the phone down.

# 11

The next day I sent Cody packing with a letter of recommendation and a personal note about how I had enjoyed his company and my decision to let him go was not personal but monetary. He didn't seem too choked up about leaving, giving me the suspicion that he was meant for bigger things than guarding a middle-aged asthmatic lady.

I told Jake to pack up too, but he refused, even after I threatened to call the police.

"Call the police. You'll just look silly," he answered defiantly. "I have a signed contract, so I'm staying until your daughter relieves me. I'm more scared of her than of you."

"Fine," I said, "but I'm calling the shots now."

"Yeah, right," Jake chuckled, as he meandered to the pool to swim his daily laps. Like me, he loved water.

I took Jake's car keys from his bureau, as he had hidden the keys to my car, and sneaked out with my purse. I got in easily and started the car, but flooded it in my excitement to escape.

I turned the key again and pressed on the pedal until a wet tanned arm reached in and pulled out the key.

"Where're you going?" asked Jake pleasantly but I could tell that he was angry. Water dripped down the door panel.

"I have more people to see regarding Jamie Dunne."

"You know you're not allowed to drive."

"My license is current."

"The doctors say you are not to drive any type of vehicle regardless if it is a car, tractor, bicycle, go-cart or snow sled. You are not even allowed to ride a pony yet, so don't even think you can ride one of those old nags of yours into town."

"I'm not Miss Daisy," I bristled, "and I don't want to be driven around."

"No, you're not. She was nice."

"She was a cranky old harridan."

"So are you. Now, I am going to finish my laps. Then after I shave and shower, I will drive you anywhere you want to go."

"I feel like I'm in a prison. I deserve to be treated with respect," I complained, tears threatening to spill over.

"Boss Lady, I respect you."

"Really? Why do you argue with me all the time?"

"Because it's fun. It's like crossing swords with a master."

"And you're bored?"

"And I'm bored," agreed Jake. "This is not the most exciting assignment. You're the only thing that makes it interesting."

"So you are an adrenaline junkie."

"Guess so."

"I know from first hand that too much adrenaline can kill you."

"Was that how the dude in your bee yard died? Too much excitement?"

"Something like that. So you know about Richard Pidgeon?"

"Franklin just couldn't wait to tell me the juicy details of how you pissed off that cop, O'nan. Come on now. Look, I'm getting chilled standing half-naked here." He opened the car door and motioned for me to get out.

Reluctantly I followed Jake into the house. I waited patiently for him until he finally emerged from his room smelling like a spring day. He placed my hand on his arm and smiled. "You'll be good now? Honest Injun?" he asked.

"Honest Injun," I said, returning his smile.

Jake gently escorted me outside.

# 12

The Golden Sun Vineyard was not open for business, but I knocked on the door anyway. Maybe someone was in the office. Minutes later, an elderly man with white hair and striking golden eyes opened the door slightly, peering out. His eyes widened slightly at the sight of Jake and myself. "Can I help you?" he asked. His voice was rich and velvety.

"Mr. Peterson. My name is Josiah Reynolds. I'm a friend of the Dunne family. May I talk with you for just a minute?" Jake bumped me from behind. "And this is my associate, Jake Dosh."

Mr. Peterson stepped out and closed the door.

"Is there somewhere we can sit and talk?" I asked, wiggling my cane.

"There's a pretty bench over there right in the sun."

"That would be good." I followed him over.

"I think I'll walk to the river," announced Jake.

Mr. Peterson started to object, but Jake was already heading down a path. He turned his attention to me. "Your name seems familiar. Do I know you?"

"I'm the lady a cop tried to pin a murder on and then threw off the cliff when it didn't stick."

Peterson's golden eyes quickly took in my cane, hearing aid and fading scars on my face. "I hope it hasn't been too awful for you," he said with compassion.

"It has its days, Mr. Peterson," I replied. "The reason that I'm here is that Jamie Dunne's aunt is a good friend of mine. She and the boy's mother are uneasy about Jamie's death and just want some questions answered so they can put this behind them."

"'Tis shameful that poor boy drowning so young." He shifted uncomfortably. "I hope Sarah Dunne's not blaming me."

"Oh, no sir. Did you know the Dunnes very well?"

"Sarah, I knew to talk to. The boy only by sight. Once in a while I'd see him kayaking past our place. He'd always wave."

"I hear you are putting out a special wine this year."

Peterson beamed. "My wife and I have been working on this for ten years, but we finally tracked down the variety of grapes that were planted in the first commercial winery in the United States, 1799. A hand-blown commemorative glass bottle will be sold to the public for a mere $200 per bottle."

"And this winery was on your property?"

"I traced old deeds, letters, maps, ledgers; anything I could get my hands on. There's no doubt about it that this was the site of the original US commercial winery."

"How exciting that must be for you."

"I know Sarah thought her winery was the first. She's got some evidence to support that, but my information is just more substantial than hers. Still, I feel bad. That's why we included Silver Creek Vineyard on our riverboat tour this summer. We want to be good neighbors."

"I live east of you on the river."

"Is that so."

"I like the river quiet, undisturbed. It seems like you are going to be opening a new segment of tourism."

"I love the river too. People ought to know what a wonderful resource we have right in our own back yard. We need to keep the river clean and healthy."

Laughing I said, "I don't want them to know about it because they'll destroy it."

Peterson politely returned my smile.

"Did you or anyone on your place ever have bad words with the Dunnes?"

"Sarah was always friendly and jumped at the chance to be on the river tour. As for the boy, I never spoke to him. Like I said, just waved."

"The autopsy report stated that there was gasoline residue on his clothing. I understand that there was a fire here that night as well."

"Someone torched the lower vineyard."

"Were the vines destroyed?"

"Some, but not many. Just scorched them slightly. Whoever lit them on fire was an amateur. Didn't know how to set a fire properly. The gasoline just burned off and the fire quit. The vines were still wet from a rain we had had that morning."

"Do you think that Jamie started those fires?"

Mr. Peterson's brow furrowed. "Don't rightly know, but it looks that way."

"Was there ever any evidence tying Jamie to the fires?"

"The county sheriff took a report and left the cans here."

"What cans?"

"The gasoline cans found near the vines. I still have them. There wasn't much destruction so nothing much was done about it. Just petty vandalism. We didn't hear about Jamie Dunne's death until several days later. The city police investigated that. I never got a call from either division tying the two together, but I happen to think they're connected."

"Mr. Peterson, may I have the cans? You have my word of honor, whatever I find, you'll be the first to know."

Mr. Peterson thought quietly for a moment. "All right. Since you had trouble with the law, you know what it's like to have suspicion thrown on you. I don't think you'd do me wrong. But you tell me first, and I will give permission if I want that information given out. Deal?"

I held out my hand. "Deal." We shook hands.

Peterson left and returned in a few moments with two gasoline cans and a bag. Unfortunately, he had picked up the cans with his hands. *Oh dear.*

I opened the trunk to the car and had him lay the articles down.

By that time, Jake was walking back up the path. He waved to me.

I got in the front seat of the car and rolled down the window, waiting for Jake to get in.

Mr. Peterson leaned in. "Sarah doesn't think I had anything to do with that boy's death, does she?"

"Of course not."

Mr. Peterson looked relieved.

I didn't offer that Irene Meckler thought he had something to do with it.

He stood in the driveway, waving goodbye with a puzzled look on his face as Jake pulled out.

We waited until we had left the property to exchange notes. "What do you think?" asked Jake.

"If Mr. Peterson had anything to do with Jamie's death, I'd be surprised. He seems like the salt-of-the-earth type. He gave me what was supposed to have been the gasoline cans used for the fire . . . and a waterproof boat bag. What did you find?"

"I walked all the way down to the river. The spring rains have washed everything away. I didn't find anything but this." He held out a cheap greenish ring and part of a silver chain.

"Looks like a girl's ring," I said. "I'll show it to Sarah and Irene and see if they recognize it."

Jake dropped the jewelry into a baggie I held for him. I put the bag in my purse and reclined the back of my seat, closing my eyes. The next thing I knew Jake was rapping on the car window. I must have fallen asleep. I slowly got out of the car while he checked the house. I waited outside until he gave me the okay to enter. Tired, I went straight to bed. I was sleeping my life away, it seemed.

\*

Awakening to savory aromas filtering through my bedroom, I followed the smells until I came to the Nakashima table, where Irene and Jake were having a dinner of country fried steak smothered in thick brown gravy, mashed potatoes and creamed corn washed down with some Old Spears Vineyard's Fayette Rose wine.

Baby was sitting with his muzzle on the table, hoping to irritate Jake into putting a steak in his bowl. He licked his muzzle and then the table with his long, drooling tongue.

Both Irene and Jake ignored him as Jake told Irene of his trip to the Trail of Tears memorial in Hopkinsville.

"Hello sleepyhead," said Irene. "Jake's been telling me about his trip."

I scooted my chair to the table as Jake went to fix me a plate. Sneaking a quick sip of Irene's wine, I looked guiltily around to see if Jake had seen. Irene pinched me.

"Stop it," I hissed playfully.

Jake returned and placed a plate before me. It consisted of a cold salad with a lump of pureed tuna fish in the middle. "When am I going to eat country steak?" I whined.

"When you're down to your college weight and can eat a good piece of meat without throwing up," rasped Jake, crisply snapping a napkin on his lap.

"Can I at least have some corn?"

"Corn gives you hives."

"I'm hungry."

"That's good, honey. That shows that you're gaining your health back. When you were in Key West, we had to beg you to eat," said Irene. Hoping to distract me, Irene continued. "Jake was telling me some fascinating stories about Choctaw history. Did you know that Choctaws raised $710 to send to Ireland for victims of the potato famine in 1847? That was a lot of money back then and that was after Andrew Jackson had taken their farms. Can you imagine what a sacrifice it was to donate $710?"

Jake took up the story. "In 1992 to commemorate the gift, an Irish contingent came here and rewalked the Choctaw Trail of Tears backwards from Broken Bow, Oklahoma five hundred miles to Nanih Waiya, Mississippi. I walked part of it myself and made friends with some of them. So if they are in the states, we meet if we can. We rendezvoused this time in Hopkinsville."

"Why would the Choctaws travel all that way up north when they needed to go west?" asked Irene.

"No, I was at the Cherokee Trail of Tears memorial. The Choctaws went by the route I just told you, but the result was the same. Lots of innocents died."

"Have you visited the Kentucky Choctaw Academy site between Georgetown and Frankfort?" I asked.

"That's near me," piped Irene. "What is it?"

"It *was* a school for Choctaw boys. Richard Johnson, ninth vice president of the United States, ran it. Actually, a lot of Indian boys got a good education there."

"Yeah, run by the man who killed Tecumseh. I'm sure he did it out of the goodness of his Christian heart. More like the goodness of his pocketbook," complained Jake bitterly.

"Now, now. Let's not get out the war drums. If I remember my history correctly, the Indians did their fair share of bloodletting," I replied.

Jake started to heatedly respond but thought better of it. "It was our land, not yours," he rebutted quietly.

He turned to Miss Irene. "Did you know that there was a Shawnee village right here in central Kentucky? Eskippakithiki. When Columbus landed, there were thousands of people living in Kentucky but by Daniel Boone's time, there were no natives living here."

"What happened?" asked Irene.

"Disease brought on by the Europeans. It is estimated that perhaps four out of every five Native Americans died between 1492 and 1750 due to European diseases."

"Oh dear," murmured a startled Irene.

131

"That happens when populations shift," I interjected. "If you remember your history, Europe almost got wiped out by the plague several times – when the Black Death came to Europe aboard infected ships."

Jake started to say something but I interrupted, "And the Native American gave the European syphilis."

"That's just a theory," replied Jake heatedly.

"My point is that bacteria and viruses act without personal feelings. They just do their thing and people pay the price. Everyone pays the price."

"I have a little Native American blood," interjected Irene.

"You do not," I protested. "You're German, through and through."

"I'll have you know that my grandmother on my daddy's side was part Cherokee."

"Everybody in Kentucky has a grandmother who is part Cherokee," I said, picking at the tuna. "It's the state joke."

"Well, I actually do. You don't know everything, missy," sputtered Irene.

"I bet you don't know that Simon Kenton deliberately misidentified Tecumseh's body so the whites wouldn't mutilate it."

"That name is familiar but I can't place 'im."

"For goodness sakes, Irene, pick up a history book once in a while."

Irene harrumphed.

Jake cut in. "We would have had ice cream for dessert, Irene, but someone ate an entire gallon of it," he said, looking accusingly in my direction, causing me to turn and stare accusingly at Baby.

"Bad boy, Baby," I said.

Baby cocked his head, looking at me curiously.

Irene laughed. "Shame on you, blaming that poor animal."

During the rest of dinner, Jake regaled us with tall tales of growing up in Oklahoma and had Irene and me in stitches. Afterwards, Jake made sure I swallowed my evening pills. Irene counted each one as I swallowed.

"Don't worry," I said to Irene. "Jake is making sure that he weans me off the cocaine before I go back to the Farmers' Market."

When finished, I took Irene into my office. She nervously worried the hem of her dress. I gave her a quick rundown of whom I had talked with so far. I showed her the raunchy magazines, the dope and the condom wrapper.

She turned pale, but she couldn't throw any light on who Jamie was seeing. "Please don't tell Sarah about this," requested Irene.

I held up the cheap ring. "Do you recognize this?"

Irene took the baggie and examined its contents. "No, never seen it before."

"I might want to take it to Sarah and see if she recognizes it."

"Okay, but don't tell her about the rest."

"What about the gasoline cans?"

Irene pulled a checkbook out of her purse and wrote a check for $2000. "See if there're any fingerprints and what other tests you deem fit."

"You'd be throwing your money away. Any fingerprints now would be degraded."

"Just try."

I pulled out the stained canvas bag.

She tentatively opened it and rummaged through it. "Oh," she said suddenly and pulled out a piece of green cloth with a partial logo of a local boys' camp. "This looks like a T-shirt that Jamie owned. I remember telling him that the shirt looked nasty and he should put it in the rag bin."

"Can you positively I.D. it?"

"No, but it sure looks like it. Same cloth. Same color."

"What about the bag?"

"Can't help you there."

Seeing that Irene was exhausted from our conversation, I wrote a receipt for the $2000. She left looking worried. It didn't look good. We now had possible evidence that tied Jamie to the fire at the Golden Sun Vineyard. From Mr. Peterson's own testimony, Jamie had the strength to paddle his kayak to the Golden Sun Vineyard and back home. The marked map, the newspaper article and the torn T-shirt identified by Irene plus the gas cans and gas residue on Jamie's clothes were building a case that Jamie had set the fire at the Golden Sun Vineyard.

Maybe Jamie hadn't been such a good boy, after all.

# 13

I no longer cooked. I couldn't stand the strain of standing needed to cook. So there was no more hot buttermilk biscuits smothered with honey, red-eye gravy over country ham, thick buckwheat pancakes, cheese grits, greasy green beans cooked with ham hock, skillet fried milk corn, baked macaroni with three different cheeses, lasagna with my homemade tomato sauce, crispy fried chicken, chilled tomatoes with just a hint of salt layered over fresh salad greens drizzled with honey dressing, blackberry cobbler, chocolate cake with cream cheese icing or my homemade peach ice cream served in frosted glass dishes. Besides, I wasn't allowed to eat any of that, so what was the point?

My food now was mostly soft, low in calories (I still needed to lose thirty pounds) and boring. So when Jake had an appointment in Versailles, I waved goodbye as he pulled out of the driveway, and then made a beeline to call Franklin.

Since I had explained to Franklin that time was on his side and not mine, he felt all so much the better about me. The anger had disappeared or at least submerged into Franklin's rather dense subconscious. I begged him to have mercy and take me to lunch. I craved real food.

An hour later Franklin arrived in his Smart Car to take me to lunch, but first I made him take me to the ferry. I wanted to talk to the captain. If anyone knew what was going on concerning the river, it would be Captain McDowell.

After parking the car in the ferry parking lot, Franklin helped me walk down the ramp and onto the ferry.

"Howdy, Miss Josiah. Heard you were back," said Captain McDowell, coming out of his little cabin. "Someone meetin' you across the river?"

"I actually came to jaw a spell with you."

"What can I do you for?"

"Nobody knows the river like you do. I need to know if anything unusual has happened in the last three months."

"Three months? I thought surely you would want to know about George Smitty's car being stolen the night you had your accident."

"I've been told that. I'm looking for something newer. Something out of place."

McDowell rubbed his weathered cheek and thought for a moment. "Well, a boy drowned on the river not too far back."

"Something else. Now think. It could be as simple as otters changing their home base."

"It's been pretty quiet lately. Rodney Tavis was complaining that someone was messing with his nets, but that was back before the boy died."

"Who is Rodney Tavis?"

"He's one of the few commercial fishermen left on the Kentucky River."

"I didn't know that there were commercial fishermen on the river."

"Just a few. Not like it used to be."

"What was happening to his nets?"

"Someone was pulling them up, taking the fish and then cutting the nets up. Those nets are expensive. It made him plumb mad."

"Anything else?"

"Heard a panther the other morning just around dawn. I know it wasn't a bobcat because the pitch was higher."

"I've heard they might be moving back in the area," I commented.

"Wouldn't that be somethin', Miss Josiah, to look up and see one of them big cats on a ledge."

"Where can I find Rodney Tavis?"

"On the river most days, but I couldn't tell you where. Don't know where he lives. A word of advice – he doesn't always abide by the law. I've had to report him several times for illegal fishing."

"Gotcha. Don't mess with his nets and don't mention your name. Thanks," I said, after handing him a jar of honey.

Captain McDowell held the jar up to the sunlight, inspecting it. After determining that the honey met his exacting standards, McDowell put the jar by his coffee mug and nodded his thanks. A driver blew his horn, letting us know he was impatient to be off across the river. I thanked the captain and left.

Franklin was waiting at the water's edge, and soon we were heading back into town to eat. I was determined to order fried chicken with the works. My body was craving deep fried meat. We arrived at my favorite greasy dive and were seated quickly. I was about to give my order to the waitress when Franklin's eyes grew wide and he said, "Let's go. I want to go to another restaurant."

Dismissing the waitress, I asked, "What's wrong?"

"Don't like it here. Wanna go somewhere else."

"Franklin?" I yelped, as he began tugging at my arm.

"Let's go!"

"Wait. Let me get my stick," I said sharply, standing up and turning to get my cane off the back of the chair.

That's when I saw her – Brannon's mistress. The woman whom Brannon loved more than me. The woman who had given birth to his second child. The woman who had taken all his wealth. The woman who was the reason I was cash poor. She was with a younger man, presumably her brother, and an older one, her father, who upon seeing me stare, leaned forward and whispered to her. She turned her head, as did a toddler following her gaze. Her expression was one of surprise, then anger and then fear. She trailed her eyes toward the toddler.

The little boy, thinking I was a friend of his mother's, waved a chicken finger at me, smiling. It was Brannon's smile. And Brannon's eyes.

"Yes, let's go. I think I'm suddenly in the mood for Chinese," I murmured, turning my back on them.

Franklin helped me out the door and we took Chinese takeout home.

With Matt and Jake joining us out on the patio by the pool, I managed to have a good time as we argued over moo goo gai pan who the actors were in *The Magnificent Seven*.

"It was not Lee Van Cleef," Franklin argued. "It was Eli Wallach who was the villain."

"It doesn't matter," said Matt, "because the greatest western was *My Darling Clementine*."

Jake interrupted, "That's because Victor Mature's in it. Personally I hate all westerns. Let's move on to another subject."

"That's because your people always lost," I said.

"They didn't in *They Died With Their Boots On*," countered Jake with a sneer.

"Oooh, that's a good one," said Franklin, grabbing a carton of fried rice. "With the dashing Errol Flynn and the always noble, but hopelessly boring Olivia de Havilland. Of course, the movie was just fantasy about

Custer. The only fact in it was that he died by the hands of the Sioux."

"No, no, you're all wrong. *Shane* is the best western ever made," I said. "Alan Ladd versus Jack Palance. Mythic, simply mythic." I imitated Brandon De Wilde crying, "Shane. Shane. Come back, Shane."

All three guys gagged as though they were going to upchuck which made me laugh. Apparently they didn't care for Alan Ladd whom they thought looked like a girl.

"Best line ever uttered by Jack Palance," stated Franklin, "was in that Billy Crystal movie. 'I shi . . .' "

"Shut up," commanded Matt. "Not when we're eating."

"Yes, please," echoed Jake. "Although, it was a pretty good line."

"Best water movie?" I asked, hoping to move the conversation along.

"*Jaws*. Hands down," said Matt.

"I thought *Dead Calm* with Nicole Kidman was pretty good," interjected Franklin, reaching for one of my spring rolls.

I slapped his hand away. No one touches my spring rolls.

Jake looked thoughtful. "What was the name of that movie where the two tourists go scuba diving and get left behind for the sharks to eat?"

"I couldn't bear to watch it," I laughed. "It was too horrible. Those poor tourists."

"The best water movie ever made was *Moby Dick* with Gregory Peck," said Franklin.

"No, it's *Jaws*," replied Matt in a voice that challenged Franklin to contradict him.

"It's *Beach Blanket Bingo*," I said. "You're all wrong."

The guys threw rice at me.

"Hey, watch the hair. Not in the hair. It's sacred."

"The sweatiest movie ever made," challenged Matt.

"That's easy," replied Jake. "*Cool Hand Luke.*"

"Never seen it," said Franklin.

The rest of us gasped.

Franklin shrugged. "What? What?"

"My turn," I said. "*Alien.*"

"Ooooh, that's a good one," answered Matt. He thought for a moment. "*The Bridge On The River Kwai.*"

"Not sweaty enough," I said. "How about *Zulu?*"

"That's a great movie," confirmed Jake. "But *Twelve Angry Men* beat it. There's not a dry armpit in the entire movie."

Franklin intervened. "*Body Heat* with Kathleen Turner."

"Oh, that's another good one," said Matt.

"If I were a woman, I would like to look like Turner in that movie," said Franklin.

"I would like to look like Rita Hayworth in *Gilda*," I announced.

"Is that the movie where she flips her hair up in a close-up?" asked Jake.

"Yeah, that scene was in *Shawshank Redemption* with Morgan Freeman," said Matt. "I would know. I have had to endure watching it many times with Miss aka Hayworth over here."

"Orson Welles said that horses sweat, men perspired, but Miss Hayworth glistened," I said.

"Is that before he dumped her for some countess?" asked Matt.

I turned toward Franklin. "You've never seen *Cool Hand Luke* really?"

He shook his head. "I've never seen a Paul Newman picture."

"I thought you said you have seen every picture ever made?"

"Not when it comes to Paul Newman."

"But he's an American institution . . . an icon," said Matt. "How could you not?"

Jake chimed in. "Never seen *Hud*?"

"Nope"

"*Cat On A Hot Tin Roof*?"

"Nada."

"*Butch Cassidy And The Sundance Kid*?"

"Nyet."

"*The Sting*?"

"No way."

Jake slumped back in his chair. "How is that possible living in American culture and not seeing a Paul Newman movie? That's like never eating ice cream. Even we Choctaws have caught a Paul Newman movie, now and then."

"You're lying, Franklin," I said. "I can tell."

Franklin gave us a cheeky grin.

We dumped our drinks over his head and pushed him in the pool. Franklin reached up and pulled Matt in. Jake jumped in while I sat at the patio table watching the boys play.

Their antics made me forget seeing that woman at the restaurant. I even managed to push back thoughts of that little boy with Brannon stamped all over him. I would deal with that later.

At this very moment, I wanted to enjoy my friends, my companions, my band of brothers. They had not abandoned me. They had stuck to me like Ruth to Naomi.

Nothing else mattered.

# 14

Late next morning, Jake and I "borrowed" Lady Elsmere's boat again. It was the first day of the Butterfly tour, so I figured she would be too busy to notice its absence. Besides, I wanted out of the house. I didn't want to watch people snoop at my things or gape at me. I left the house in the capable hands of Charles, Lady Elsmere's butler, and his middle-aged daughters, Bess and Amelia.

Jake had procured a guide map of the river, so Jamie's movements on that fateful night could be retraced from the police report.

Charles, loving the fact that we were pinching his boss's boat, donated a picnic basket, full of tasty delights with an ice chest full of cold drinks including little baby bottles of champagne.

Franklin, having eavesdropped on our plans the night before, showed up dressed in canvas deck shoes, white cotton pants with a navy stripe down the side, matching navy sailor's shirt and a dandy little red hat. Of course, he brought Baby with him. It took both Franklin and Jake to carry Baby onto the boat.

Irritated that Franklin had crashed our outing, Jake told Franklin that he would have to mind Baby. As if to impress Franklin with the importance of our mission, Jake jerked his Glock out from his shoulder holster, dropping the clip and then reinserting it with a manly thrust.

In response, Franklin whipped out his binoculars.

Ignoring them both, Baby went to sleep as I sat on the backbench going through the basket to see what there was to eat.

Starting down the river, Jake put *Merle Haggard's Greatest Hits,* which he had pulled from CDs scattered around the captain's chair, in the CD player.

Franklin groaned, "Got any Gwen Stefani?"

Stuffing my mouth full of crustless cucumber and cream cheese sandwiches, I opened the report on Jamie's death and read the details out loud while Jake scoured the river map trying to find the landmarks mentioned in the report.

"Like old times," commented Franklin, putting his arm around me and giving a hug. "The three of us on a boat."

"Hardly like Key West," I said. "But I wouldn't want to miss this. Spring in Kentucky is beautiful."

All the wild dogwoods were in full bloom and, like an impressionist painter's palette, the limestone cliffs were dotted with green and white.

"We're here," Jake said, pointing to the map. Tracing his finger along the map, "There is Silver Creek Vineyard, Firstvineyard, and then according to the report, we follow the river to Lock 8 where Jamie's body was found washed up on the north side of the river. Golden Sun Vineyard is located west of where the body was found."

He read the *Kentucky River Guide* brochure. "According to this," Jake quoted, "a Jean Dufour selected land belonging to a John Hazlerigg and started the first commercial vineyard and winery in the United States, 1799. The company was named Firstvineyard. In 1804 he shipped two kegs to President Jefferson. A spring frost killed all the grape vines in 1809 and Dufour closed the winery and moved to Indiana." He read some more. "Peterson may be right. It says here that in early the 1900s, a George McQuerry was quoted in the *Jessamine Journal* as saying, 'the Firstvineyard was on a hill slope on the Kentucky River just below the mouth of Sugar Creek which was about 1 ½ miles below Lock 8.'"

"The Silver Creek Vineyard is too far east on the river to match that description and in another county," I replied. "Let's look at the facts. Jamie had gasoline on his clothes. He was a devoted son, by all accounts. Perhaps he thought that the resurrection of Firstvineyard would seriously hurt his mother's business."

"And being only fifteen and teenage-stupid, thought that burning the grapevines would stop Peterson's rivalry with his mother," continued Franklin.

"He's a big strong boy, paddles undetected to the vineyard, starts the fires and leaves. That would explain why the fires didn't do much damage. He was inexperienced in setting fires and the vines were wet," Jake mused.

"He gets back to his kayak and, in his hurry to get away, has his accident. Panics, because it's night and the alarm at the vineyard has been raised. Hits his head and drowns," I said.

"Sounds plausible," commented Franklin.

"Then why does Irene have such strong feelings about this?" I asked.

Jake shrugged. "Can't accept the fact Jamie's dead. She's looking for a scapegoat."

"I've always found her to be a sensible and fair person," I said. "I have faith in her common sense. She says she can't sleep at night. That she feels Jamie pulling on her."

"Creepy," said Franklin, his deep blue eyes blinking.

"I agree, Franklin," I said. "Very creepy. It's not like Irene to be imagining things."

"Nonsense," replied Jake, slowing the boat. "It's just part of the grieving process."

"Then why are you helping me if you think there has been no foul play?" I asked.

"Because where you go, I go."

I cocked my head at him, but said nothing. His words stirred something inside me.

"It's my job. You're my job," repeated Jake.

"Oh," I murmured, disappointed.

Franklin handed Jake a plate of sandwiches and other treats with a cold soda before he loaded his own plate. He sat beside me happily munching away while making tick marks in his bird book. He rested his feet on Baby. "Look, Josiah, a green heron," he cried as he made his mark. "My goal is to see at least twenty different bird species today. Oh my goodness. Look! Look! Two ospreys!"

Both Jake and I turned to see the graceful fish-eating bird soar into the distance while another one peered out from a large extended twig nest located in a dead tree.

"Look for bald eagles. They might be migrating through here," I said, closing my eyes to rest for a moment.

"This is just too cool," giggled Franklin. "Oh, oh, oh, a kingfisher!"

"Boss Lady, we are at Silver Creek Vineyard," announced Jake.

"Pull in, please. I want to talk with Sarah," I said.

Jake pulled up to the dock and tied the boat up.

I got out with his help, and we walked up the path while Franklin and Baby waited in the boat.

Sarah had been sitting on her house deck talking with Bloomie when we pulled up. She waved us onto the deck. I plopped into a chair, catching my breath.

Bloomie brought some iced tea.

"Wait a minute, Bloomie," I said as she tried to make an exit. "I want you to look at something."

"What's going on?" asked Sarah.

"We are retracing Jamie's journey according to the police report, but first I wanted to ask you both something." I pulled out the ring and chain that Jake had found at the Golden Sun Vineyard. "Do either of you recognize this?"

Taking the ring, Sarah turned it over in her palm. "I don't think so. No, I don't recognize it." She handed it to Bloomie.

"No," said Bloomie flatly, handing it quickly back to me while averting her eyes.

I gave her a curious look and noticed she was pale. Also her ankles were swollen and the fabric around her breast shirt buttons was straining.

"Okay, just wanted to check," I said.

"Where did you find it?" asked Sarah.

"On Golden Sun's beach near where Jamie was found."

I looked again at Bloomie. A rose flush was creeping up her neck.

There was a pause among us.

"Well, I thought this might be a clue," I said.

"'Fraid I can't help you," said Sarah.

"Jake, why don't you go and start the boat." I turned toward Sarah. "Thanks Sarah. I'll be in contact. Bloomie, can you help me down the path?"

Bloomie glanced at Sarah, who nodded yes.

I smiled, putting my hand on Bloomie's arm as we started down the slope to the boat dock. Taking little baby steps, I forced Bloomie to slow down.

"Bloomie," I said, looking at the river. "I found a condom wrapper under Jamie's bed when I was here last." I could feel her arm tense under my hand. "By everyone's account, he didn't have a girlfriend."

Stopping on the pathway, I turned Bloomie toward me. "Did you feel grateful to Jamie because he got you a job here? Perhaps he asked you to somehow show your gratitude?"

Bloomie's soulful eyes filled with tears as she pulled away.

"Don't worry," I said. "Mrs. Dunne has gone back into the house. She can't hear you."

"Please don't tell anyone," Bloomie begged. "I was grateful . . . but it wasn't as you suggested. I wanted to. I loved Jamie. I wanted to be his girlfriend."

"Did he feel the same way about you?"

"I don't know, but he was always kind to me. That was enough . . . for then."

"Is this ring yours?"

She nodded her head. "Yes, I gave it to him as a good luck piece."

"It must have meant something to him as he was wearing it the night he died."

The teenage girl looked gratefully at me.

"How far along are you, Bloomie?"

Her button of a mouth dropped. "How do you know?" she asked, stealing another glance at the house.

"I can just tell. I don't mean to be insensitive, but if you were using protection then how . . ."

"We didn't always. When he ran out of condoms, he was too embarrassed to ask for more."

"Where did he get them?"

Bloomie hung her head. "From some guy at church."

"Church?"

"Yeah, the church he and his mom went to. He had a friend there. Never told me his name, but this guy helped him out. But their friendship went sour, so Jamie quit hanging around him."

"What happened?"

"He kept gettin' in Jamie's business. It made Jamie feel weird, like somethin' wasn't right with this guy."

"I think I know who it is."

Bloomie bit her lip while shoving her thick, doughy hands in her pockets. She wouldn't look at me.

"Does Mrs. Dunne know?"

Bloomie shook her head.

"Are you going to tell her?"

"Don't know. Haven't decided what I'm going to do. I'm in a world of trouble, that's for sure."

"What about your folks?"

She snorted derisively. "Useless. I can't wait till next year when I'm eighteen and can get away from them."

"I can't tell you what to do. I don't know your circumstances, but once you decide, I can help refer you to an agency or to a home that can help."

"You won't tell Mrs. Dunne?"

It was my turn to shake my head. "As much as it pains me to keep this from Sarah, this is your decision. You must make the choice of what to do. If she is to be told, then it must be you who does the telling," I said. "You're now an adult. You took up adult pleasures and now you must make adult decisions regarding the consequences."

The young girl's face quivered at my words.

I put my arm around her. "I know. I know. Love makes a person do crazy things. But don't wait long. If I could tell that you're having a baby, she will too very soon." I handed the ring back to Bloomie. "Take care, Bloomie, and good luck to you."

She wiped away a tear, putting the ring in her pocket. I could tell that the fact Jamie was carrying the ring when he died meant a great deal to her. It was possibly the only evidence of his feelings for her. Bloomie would never know the truth for sure.

Growing impatient, Franklin had already started the boat and I barely made it back in when he started to ease the boat away from the dock.

"Did they recognize it?" asked Franklin, over his shoulder.

"No, they hadn't seen it before," I replied. I caught Jake studying Bloomie walking up the pathway to the Dunne's house. He turned and caught my glance.

"Where's the ring now?" Jake asked.

"I gave it to Bloomie."

Looking smug, he said, "Thought so. Her waist has thickened since the last time we saw her." He waited for me to comment.

"It's none of our business," I replied.

"Are you sure it has nothing to do with his death?"

"I'm not sure of anything, but I doubt it. Bloomie's just a poor, frightened teenage girl with no one to help her. Until we know that it does, her condition does not exist for us."

"I can play it cool." He reflected, "The beautiful Jamie and the plain Bloomie, huh."

He shook his head and went to stand with Franklin, giving me time to reflect. *Poor Bloomie. I had rarely seen a young person so alone.*

We continued down the river close to the south bank looking for anything unusual when we came to a pool of orange disks floating in the water.

Jake pulled a disk up with my cane only to find it attached to a complex fishing net.

"These must be commercial fishing nets," said Jake.

"Yeah, but it is after the deadline for commercial fishing in this pool. These must be illegal traps," I commented, counting the number of disks.

A small motorboat careened out of the shadows, criss-crossing the water to face our boat. The three of us turned to face a scraggly-looking man training a shotgun on us.

"Hey man, what do you think you're doing?" asked Jake. He slowly inched toward his shoulder holster.

"Be still, Pilgrim," ordered the stranger. "Keep your hands where I can see them. I'd hate to have an accident with this hair trigger."

"Are you Rod Tavis?" I asked.

The man blinked at the sound of his name. "Who you be?"

"I'm Mrs. Reynolds. This is Jake and Franklin."

"Whatcha doin' messin' wit' my nets?"

"We saw the orange disks floating and were just curious. We meant no harm. Please lower the gun. It is making me very nervous and I need to sit down. My leg is bad."

Tavis lowered his shotgun and propelled his boat closer to ours. "Sorry, Miss, but somebody's been messin' with my nets. They're my livin' and I gots to protect them."

"What are you trying to catch?"

"Catfish. People love fried catfish."

"I know I do," I replied, while handing Tavis a bottle of water.

He reached up with a grubby hand, nodding his thanks.

I noticed a prison tattoo on his wrist. "Have you seen any eagles this year?"

"Saw one migrating yesterday. Stop for a few hours to fish and then moved on."

"I wish they would stay," I said wearily.

"They're awful pretty."

"Do you fish just in this pool?" I asked innocently, now handing him several of Charles' tea sandwiches.

"I fish all over.  Got to.  Don't want to overfish."

Jake interjected, "They really should reopen all the river locks."

Pulling a bandana from around his yellow scrawny neck, Tavis wiped his creased face.  "No money in the budget and not enough traffic on the river to justify it.  Well, that's the way it goes."

"Were you on the river the day that boy drowned?"

"I'm on the river every day."

"I thought perhaps you might have seen him."

Tavis blinked while swatting an early gnat.  "Nope, can't say that I did.  Don't go out on the river at night.  Never saw him."  He swatted away a dragonfly darting between us.  "Sorry to have scared you folks, but I've gots to git on down the river and check more of my nets."

"Nice to have met you," I said.

"Same here.  Thanks for the refreshments."  Tavis revved up his motor and was soon making his way against the current.

"Well, that was interesting," I said.

Franklin looked down at his pants.  "I don't need to pee anymore.  Why are people always pulling a gun on me?"

Jake stifled a laugh.  "Don't worry, the wind will dry you out soon.  Just stay downwind from us, okay."

"And don't sit on the cushions," I cautioned, "or June will be all over me.  What's that obnoxious odor, Daaarlin'?"  I mimicked in her Tallulah Bankhead voice.

Franklin grinned.  "We can always blame Baby."

The three of us glared at Baby, who had not even lifted his head when Tavis had pulled a shotgun on us. He was sleeping soundly. I stepped over him to get a beach towel for Franklin, which he wrapped around himself.

We finished our trip, canvassing both sides of the river and the east side of Lock 8. Nothing. Daunted, we returned home finding June, aka Lady Elsmere, on the dock waiting for us.

She was wearing a faded safari bushmaster outfit complete with several evening diamond bracelets to finish the ensemble.

Charles was standing behind her with a little smile on his lips. He was holding a pith helmet attached to a natty little veil.

Franklin jumped out of the pontoon and tied it up.

Jake put me and the food baskets over the side before he double-checked that the boat was left shipshape.

"Hello, June," I said, exaggerating the limp in my walk. "Sahib going to hunt simba today?"

"You're not going to joke your way out of stealing my boat. This is going to cost you, Josiah," announced June.

"I intend to pay for the gas."

"I am giving a dinner party next weekend."

"No. No. NO! I hate your dinner parties. Remember what happened after the last one."

"That had nothing to do with me. If you had stayed with me, then O'nan would have tried to just kill that boy over there," she said, pointing to Franklin. "Oh, my goodness, did you have that canine monster on my brand new boat?"

156

Baby padded over to June and stuck his muzzle in her ancient crotch. *Great.*

Franklin pulled him away, apologizing.

It didn't rattle her. June continued, "I will send a car for you at seven sharp." Turning, she got into her Bentley.

Charles retrieved the basket and ice chest. He was mumbling under his breath. I could tell that this was the first time he had heard of a dinner party.

As soon as they pulled off, Franklin jumped in front of me. "I'm going with you. I missed out last time. It's my turn to go to Lady Elsmere's." Touching his bad shoulder, he blurted, "I deserve to go after what I've been through."

Jake pushed him out of the way. "You're not going anywhere, Sport. I am going to be the Boss Lady's escort."

Franklin snorted, "As if you own a suit, let alone a tuxedo. Don't you need to be outside patrolling the grounds or something like that, protecting people?"

"It doesn't matter," I interrupted, "'cause I'm not going."

"NOT GOING?" they both groused. "YOU HAVE TO GO! We want to see the house."

"Goodness, I had no idea this meant so much to the two of you to be invited to that old biddy's home."

"Pick one of us," demanded Franklin.

"No way. I'm not going."

Jake pulled out a coin. "Call it," he said, as he tossed it in the air.

"Heads," called Franklin.

Jake caught and flipped it on his forearm. Both peered carefully as Jake lifted his hand. "Aiyee, tails. I'm going." He did a little victory dance.

"Two out of three," begged Franklin.

"No, man. You lost fair and square."

"Come on, paper, scissors, rock?"

Jake shook his head.

"It's not fair!" wailed Franklin.

Life's not fair. My thoughts flickered back to Bloomie and Jamie.

Life sure hadn't been fair to them.

# 15

The next afternoon, I heard Matt calling for me throughout the house. Not being able to move, I knew he would find me eventually. He did. Poking his head in my bedroom, he caught me squeezed between Franklin and Jake on my bed watching a movie on my new big-screen TV.

Baby was lying on the end of the bed with our feet propped up on him. The two barn cats were ensconced asleep on Jake's lap while Franklin happily munched popcorn.

We were watching the film noir classic, *Kiss Of Death* with Victor Mature and Richard Widmark, whose performance of the psycho, Tommy Udall, gave Jack Nicholson and Heath Ledger a run for their money for similar performances.

Jake looked at the screen and then at Matt. "Hey, he really does look like Victor Mature."

Matt gave us an odd look before announcing, "Bees are swarming!"

In my struggle to climb over Franklin, I knocked over the bowl of popcorn and poked Baby in the ribs with my feet. The cats flew off Jake's lap with an angry screech. I hobbled outside to the golf cart where I stored my bee equipment. Of course, I had put swarm catchers everywhere, but honeybees are notorious for not doing what they are supposed to. I put on a veil and gloves, but shunned the complete beesuit, as swarming bees are usually easy to handle. Matt jumped in the cart and we rattled down the gravel road into the horse pasture where Matt had spotted bees balled into a lump in a tree. The buzzing of the bees kept the horses at bay.

Thirty thousand bees, forming a cluster, hung from a tree limb about fifteen feet up from the ground. I needed to work quickly before they took off to their permanent home.

Swarming is how honeybees proliferate. The hive gets too crowded in the spring, so the old queen leaves with some of her workers while a new queen takes over the hive. If a beekeeper can catch the swarm, she has a new bee colony.

Matt and I laid a white sheet under the clump of bees. Matt pulled out a nuc and installed two frames smeared with thick crystallized honey. He then positioned himself under the clump of bees holding up the plastic box, while I took a broom and gently tried to knock the bee ball into it. Part of the clump did find their way into the nuc, but the other part fell on the sheet. Immediately the bees began to fly back up to the branch where they had last smelled their queen. Matt brought down the nuc onto the sheet and pushed the confused clump into the box and closed the lid. I opened the small bottom entrance of the nuc. Bees, crawling on the sheet, made a beeline to the nuc and obediently entered.

I waited until escaped bees made another ball on the tree and then again knocked it down onto the sheet. Some immediately got the idea and joined their sisters in the nuc. Others seemed confused and flew in circles around the box. I put some honey around the entrance as bait. Eventually all the bees would succumb to the nuc. I would pick it up in the morning when they were calm and take the bees to an empty hive body where they would be installed in their new homes.

Leaving the nuc on the sheet, Matt and I toured the farm looking for more bee swarms. I would do this twice a day now for several weeks until the swarming season was over. If I were lucky, the bees would be happily installed in swarm boxes which I could transfer to hive bodies. Or the bees could be in a tree, fifty feet up and out of my reach. That was a loss of income to me and a loss to Kentucky, which needed every honeybee it had. Swarms that go off on their own usually die.

We found another small swarm of bees on a fence post. I put crystallized honey on a frame and with a soft brush, brushed them onto the frame. They protested until they smelled the honey. Too busy eating; they stayed on the frame as I put it in a nuc box, which is nothing more than a portable home. I kept doing this with frames until most of the bees were off the post and munching contently on a thick cream of honey. I closed the top of the nuc box and opened the side entrance. Putting honey around the entrance, I then brushed off the remaining bees from the fence post and hoped they had the sense to go with their sisters. Again, I left them to do their bee thing. I would pick up the nuc in the morning. I didn't know if this swarm would survive. I hadn't seen a queen. If in two weeks I didn't find brood in the hive, I would combine the bees with a larger hive so they could thrive.

Leaning against the golf cart, I pulled off my veil. Matt stored the equipment. We both grinned at each other.

"I haven't seen you smile like that in about two years," Matt reflected. "It's nice."

"Matt, I actually feel happy. I didn't think I would ever feel that way again. If I were a cat, I'd be purring."

"If you will wait until tomorrow evening, when I get home from work, I'll help you install the bees."

"You got a deal there, good buddy."

"Hey, can we come over?" yelled Franklin. Both Franklin and Jake had followed us, watching at a respectable distance.

I waved them over.

"That was pretty interesting," said Jake, "but better you than me. Bees give me the creeps."

"That's because they are not indigenous to North America. Europeans brought them over. Your people have no history with them."

"Huh?" responded Jake. "Still, what you did was impressive and I'm looking forward to eating the honey."

"Speaking of eating, I'm hungry," said Franklin.

"Why don't we go into town?" I suggested.

"Yeah, that sounds good," stated Franklin.

"You decide, Franklin. You're the fussiest eater of us all," I said. "Make it a casual place. I don't want to change my clothes."

We looked up to the sound of a vehicle making its way across the field. It was Shaneika, waving.

"We were just thinking of getting something to eat. Wanna come?" I asked.

"Where're you going?" she asked, climbing out of her SUV.

"Franklin's going to decide," said Matt.

"How about eating at a restaurant on the river? It's such a pretty afternoon," said Shaneika.

"That's the ticket. Let's all go, right now," said Franklin, snapping his fingers. "I get to ride shotgun."

We piled into Shaneika's SUV with Franklin riding in front, making Shaneika crazy with his driving advice while we headed toward the river to eat fried catfish, baked potato loaded with butter and sweet iced tea. And I was going to do my best to eat them with my new teeth.

Life was good to live again.

*

The next morning I checked on the beehives. It was the first day I was allowed to venture forth alone. Of course, like any new mother giving her child independence for the first time, there were conditions from Jake. I had to take the golf cart. I had to take the walkie-talkie. I had to check in every 15 minutes with the walkie-talkie. I could only stay out for an hour and a half. I could not leave the property. I could not talk to strangers. The list was endless but let me go, he did.

I first went to the main bee yard and from the golf cart observed the entrance of each beehive. I was looking for good flying patterns of the workers, guards at the entrances and a lack of flies. Flies, hanging around an entrance, were a sign of trouble.

Driving close to the back of a hive, I placed a bottle of honey with a note saying: "Dear Mr. Goren, Next time you see me, please say hello. Running off scares me. Being a man of God, you understand my circumstances are strained this year. Once I am better, you can return to being a hermit. But for now, have compassion and be a neighbor. Don't creep me out. It will make me run into a tree trying to get away. This honey is a welcome-to-the-neighborhood gift. Mrs. Reynolds. PS: Thank you for the walking stick. I am using it right now."

I placed both the honey and note in a transparent waterproof bag and left them on the hive top held down by a rock. Seeing that things were cool in the bee world, I went to check on the nucs.

There was activity around the bluebird boxes that Shaneika had put up on the fence posts. Bright blue bullets of color flashed out of the boxes before winging off. It turned out that Miss Shaneika Mary Todd was an avid bird watcher and secret animal lover. It was only humans that she couldn't abide. Perhaps she turned sour on the human race after she became a lawyer. I would have to needle that information out of her.

"No!" I cried. The golf cart jerked to a halt. The nuc, with thirty thousand bees, was smashed and laying on its side. All the frames were shattered and thrown to the ground. They were covered with dead bees. Those who survived flew haplessly above the broken nuc.

Having more nucs in the back of the cart, I remained calm getting out of the cart. It wouldn't help the situation if I panicked and fell while getting out. I prepared a new nuc and spread out a white sheet on top of the broken frames, placing the new one on top of it. I pinned a queen pheromone tube inside the nuc. The worker bees needed a smell to latch onto. I picked up the remains of the nuc with my new walking stick. Inside, a clump of survivors had hung on. I shook them into the new nuc box and then closed the top, opening the bottom entrance. All I could do now was wait until the evening, hoping all the surviving bees would enter the new nuc box.

Straight away, I drove to the horse pasture with the other nuc box. It too was smashed. Tears began to escape from my eyes. As my coping skills were on the same level as a toddler's now, it didn't take much for frustration to build and the waterworks to turn on. I called Jake on the walkie-talkie and, between the sobbing, told him that someone had hurt my bees.

"Don't move," Jake ordered. "I'll be right there." And he was.

After making sure I was all right, Jake sat patiently with me in the golf cart while I blew my nose.

"Could an animal have done this?"

"I guess a raccoon could have, but I have used these boxes for four years now. This is the first time anything like this has happened."

"What about a bear?"

"No bears in this part of Kentucky unless a stray just wandered through."

"Hmmmm," murmured Jake. He jumped out of the cart and with my walking stick lifted the destroyed box, pulling it toward him. A surviving bee stung him. "Hell," he uttered. "I hate bees. They're always stinging someone."

"No, they aren't," I said, defending them. "There are millions of bees on this farm and only one little girl bee has stung you in fear. Grow some, Jake."

He shook out dead bees from the crumpled box and turned it over. "Boss Lady, I wish you hadn't fired Cody."

"I can't foolishly spend my daughter's money. We're okay with just you."

"No, we're not. There are tire tracks on this box. Someone did this on purpose." He turned the box over and showed me the black marks.

My skin crawled with fear.

"It's time we return to the house. I need to make some phone calls. Sorry, but your day pass has just been revoked."

Before we returned to the house, I made Jake check on all the animals. My life had been turned upside down yet again. The Butterfly was put on lockdown and I was forbidden to leave the house, even to sit on the patio.

Creating more tension, the barn cat had given birth to a litter of kittens in my closet after pulling down a cashmere sweater to make a bed for them. For a second, I thought of pulling her tail, but Jake poked his head in the closet and grinned. "Looks like an expensive sweater she's got there." We both watched her knead the sweater until she got it just right for herself and then lay down on her side. She began to lick the still wet kittens.

I began explaining to Jake why I needed to leave my bedroom patio door open so she could go outside and catch dinner.

Jake shook his head no. "She's now an indoor cat. I will get a nice comfy box for her and her babies. I will get cat food and litter, but she stays inside or we put her and the kittens in the barn. No more doors being open. These nucs are a wakeup call. Security is going to be tighter." Jake walked toward his room.

"I don't want the smell of cat urine stinking up my closet," I whined. As I watched her clean her babies, my hard heart relented; after all, while I was fond of my cashmere sweater, it was just a sweater. I mean, how selfish can a human be to deny a new feline mother a soft bed. "Hell's bells. She came here for a reason. She feels safe. I can't kick her out now." I followed Jake into the hallway.

"All doors stay locked from now on. That's final," Jake stated before going into his room.

I returned to mine only to find a confrontation in the closet. Hearing the mews of the kittens, Baby had meandered in and hovered his massive head over the sightless kittens. "Oh Baby," I pleaded, "please don't hurt . . . or eat them," fearful that if I moved, a fight would start and Baby's massive paws would accidentally hurt the tiny kittens.

The mother was bunched in corner hissing, ready to throw herself on Baby when he lowered his huge nose. I also was ready to throw myself on him if he tried to hurt the kittens. True to his good nature though, he sniffed and then licked them with his drooling tongue. Satisfied, he lumbered past me and circled three times before lowering himself in his bed.

I sighed with relief. "We will leave you alone," I said to the mother cat. "You've had a tough day and so have I." Quietly, I closed one entrance to the closet, knowing she could get out through the bathroom door. At least, it gave her some privacy to be alone with her new family.

Dinner was a quiet affair. Neither Jake nor I spoke much. As Jake was cleaning up, I broke the silence. "How much does my daughter owe you?"

"Contract has been paid in full until October of this year."

"I guess the money is in an off-shore account?"

Jake grinned. "Something like that."

"And then?"

"It depends on many factors. One being if O'nan is found alive and caught. Another being that you're well enough to live on your own."

"Is that possible . . . my living an independent life again?"

"With certain parameters, I think it is very possible. You're very far down the road to recovery," he said, putting the dishes in the dishwasher.

I paused for a moment. I wanted to articulate my thoughts correctly, which I couldn't always do now. "Jake, I can't live like this."

Jake looked at me with alarm. "What do you mean by that?"

"I can't hide. I can't live a shallow, hidden life. If O'nan is alive and out there, then we must meet him head-on. A plan. Something. But I can't live behind locked doors with the drapes pulled."

"There's no point in being stupid either. You're in no shape to meet up with O'nan. A five-year-old girl could take you down. Don't throw your life away because you don't like restrictions."

"The French philosopher Alexis de Tocqueville, witnessing the removal of the Choctaws in 1831 from Mississippi, asked one Indian why he was leaving his home and he answered, 'To be free.' I know how that man felt. I can't live my life in the shadows. I'm always afraid. I will be paralyzed with fear if I do nothing but hide."

"If I lift the restrictions, then will you will let me teach you how to properly defend yourself? No more gimmicky electronic gates. No more watchdogs."

"I admit the watchdog idea did not turn out as I had hoped."

"That dog does nothing but sleeps and eats."

"Don't forget poops."

"And farts."

"But he was shot three times trying to help me. Doesn't that count for something?"

"Yeah, 'cause I wouldn't take three bullets for you."

"Not in the contract?"

"Nope," he said, giving me a lopsided grin. "Just heal and defend when humanly possible. I decide what is humanly possible."

"You'd take a bullet for me."

"Why is that, Boss Lady?"

"Because you like me, you really do!" I kidded.

\*

The next day I went to the bank and cashed in my last remaining money cushion – my $16,000 CD.  Then I bought a shotgun.

# 16

The following Saturday was my first day back at the Farmers' Market since last October. I had honey left over from the past summer, which I took out of my walk-in freezer and put in warming tanks. Then I put the bottles on the dashboard of any vehicle I could find to let the warm sun do the rest. Armed with my cashbox, table and chair, I was ready to face the crowds. Breathe in, breathe out. Breathe in, breathe out.

Seeing my regular assigned spot empty, Jake pulled the car in easily.

Matt had paid my Market fees for the season, saving my spot.

Jake placed my table under the tree along with my chair. While he pulled out the boxes of honey, I put up my sign. Bags hung from my chair, my special apron was on and my fanny was sitting comfortably. I was ready for business.

Jake went over the rules with me again. Did I have my panic button necklace on? Was there a taser in the cash box? Was there one in my pocket? Did I have my asthma spray? Was there a friend who would accompany me to the bathroom? If someone unfriendly approached me, I was to act like I was having a heart attack. So on and so on.

"I am going to take a walk around," said Jake. "I'll be back in a few moments. You might not see me, but don't worry."

"Just blend in, Jake. Try not to scare the customers," I teased, counting the change in my cash box.

"If anyone asks, what shall I tell them?"

"Say you're my nephew from Oklahoma on my father's side come to help at the farm."

"Okey dokey," Jake said, before he scrambled into the crowd.

It took me a moment to get my bearings. Everything seemed the same, but wasn't.

Farmers were looking at me out of the corners of their eyes, wondering what to do.

Miriam, the peach lady, broke the ice first. She stood with her arms akimbo and her apron pockets stuffed full of ripe peaches. "Well, look who's decided to show up," she teased. "Look, honey. I brought you the first white peaches of the season. Aren't they precious!" She took them out of her pockets to show me. My mouth watered. Noticing my cane hanging off the chair arm, she peered into my face. "Irene said you looked good. I don't know how after that terrible fall, but the Lord had mercy on you, Josiah." She squeezed my arm. "Take these here peaches. They'll help build up your strength. Let them ripen some more in the window. Gotta go – customers."

I saw her whisper to several of her customers who then made a beeline for my table and bought honey. I didn't care if they were mercy purchases. I needed the money. Bless Miriam, who was pushing customers my way.

After the initial breakthrough, there was a slow but steady stream of customers as word of my return weaved around the market. Some people stared. Some asked me for details. I pointed to my hearing aid and said I couldn't hear them. Some kept their eyes averted. Some, like the Market Manager, just came right out and told it like it was. "Well, I've seen you look worse. Now let's make a list. You've got a cane and hearing aid that I can see. Your teeth look different . . . but in a good different sort of way. You don't happen to have a peg leg under that skirt like Captain Ahab, do you?"

"Funny, Ted."

"I have my moments. Did you get the books I sent you?"

"Yes."

"Did you read them?"

"No."

"Why not?"

"Because I don't like Kafka or biographies on Kafka."

"He's the greatest writer that ever lived."

"He was an insurance agent who wrote about people turning into big bugs."

"If you're not going to enlighten your mind, I want the books back."

"I brought them."

Ted grinned.

"You're a pain in the tuckus sometimes," I accused, returning his smile.

"I knew you hated Kafka."

"I got the joke. It was that I had to lug them back to Kentucky from Key West that irritated me."

"Didn't you laugh just a bit when you opened the box?"

"I admit I did chuckle a time or two when I opened a box filled with fourteen books written by Kafka or about Kafka. You have a weird sense of humor."

"You have no idea," he said, raising an eyebrow at me.

I waved to the car. "They're in there."

"I'll come back and get them later. Right now, I need your booth fee."

Keeping my assigned spot was like buying a condo. There were yearly and daily fees. I pulled thirty from the cashbox and gave it to him. "Hey Ted."

"Yeah?"

"Is Silver Creek Vineyard a member of this market?"

"Last time I looked," he said, writing a receipt. Someone called Ted's name. He turned and waved.

"What's the story on them?" I asked.

"Sarah Dunne is Irene's sister."

"Tell me something I don't know. What about Jamie?"

"My personal feeling?" He lowered his voice. "Jamie came every Saturday with an older employee to help set up. He was not allowed to work the booth due to his age, so he worked for Irene until the Market was over and then helped pack up. Very hard-working boy, but seemed very nervous. Always watching the other wineries, checking up on them to make sure they were following the rules."

"Was Sarah having financial problems?"

"I heard that she had bank problems."

"What kind of bank problems?"

"Loan problems."

"Anything else."

"That's all I've heard. You're not sticking your nose into Jamie's death, are you? Look what happened to you trying to find out how Richard Pidgeon died."

"Just curious," I replied.

"It was curiosity that got you that limp. Leave it alone."

It seems like people were telling me that close to a year ago. If I had listened to them . . . well, the past can't be changed. I huffed, "No, it was a crazy cop trying to pin a murder rap on me that got me this limp. Go away now or I'll call your wife and tell her that you are being a jerk to me today."

"She thinks I'm wonderful and you won't be able to shake her on that. I've got her trained to ignore your complaints."

"That's something I need to fix. Is she still a rabid liberal?"

"Crazy as a loon about freedom of speech and personal rights." Ted shrugged. "What can I do? Someone taught her to read the Constitution."

Someone called Ted's name again. He swiveled and waved to them. "Come over after the Market and we'll feed you," he said. "Nothing fancy, but wifey made a chocolate cake this morning and told me to extend an invitation if I saw you."

My face brightened. "I would love to if I'm not too tired. Can I bring someone?"

"Who?"

"My nephew from Oklahoma."

Ted gave a funny look. "If that's what you want to call him, fine, but I know that you don't have a nephew from Oklahoma. Bring him along. It will give my wife someone new to torment." He then moved to the next booth.

I made more sales until the crowd began to thin out. Seeing that the sun was nearly overhead, I called Jake on the cell phone, which he immediately answered. "Can you start packing up for me?" I asked. "I need to move around. My muscles are stiffening up."

Less than a minute later, he emerged from the crowd loaded with bags of local, fresh food. "We're gonna eat good this week!" he claimed with relish.

I oohed and ahhed at each item he pulled from the bags to show me.

Fresh-picked asparagus, sweet strawberries, free-range eggs, delicate lettuce greens, several kinds of cheeses, fresh baked bread, humanely harvested whole chickens.

I wouldn't buy meat from anyone unless the animals were humanely dispatched. I wished restaurants would do the same. It was one of my pet peeves – no pun intended.

As I began to move off, he said, "Stay where I can see you."

Weaving carefully through the crowd, I made it to Irene's booth, plopping down in her extra chair. I called Jake, told him where I was and waved so he could see me. Irene wasn't there but Jefferson Davis, her husband, was. "Hey Jeff," I said, fishing out a soda pop from their ice chest.

He tipped his broad-rimmed hat. "Like your new 'do, Miss Jo."

"It is all Irene's doing."

"So I heard," he said, handing a customer a wrapper filled with spring flowers. "Thank ya kindly now. Come back now, hear." He swiveled his chair toward me. "She said you wanted to ask me some questions. Shoot."

"What did you think of Jamie?"

Jeff lifted his hat and scratched his head of graying hair, giving him time to reflect. "I was fond of him. After his daddy died, I took him fishing a lot. A baseball game now and then."

"Did you like him?"

"Yes. He was a good boy. If he had growed, he would have been a fair-minded man."

"Did Irene tell you that I found raunchy magazines under his mattress? I'm not talking Playboy, but real hardcore stuff. There was also a torn condom wrapper under his bed."

Jeff's creased face reddened. "No, she didn't, and if it was anybody else telling me this, I would call them a liar to their face. I sure didn't give him that stuff. Don't hold with it. I hope you didn't think that I would give a young boy such trash."

"I was just wondering if he talked to you about sex or girls – anything that can help me."

"We talked about school, fishing and future plans. This was a boy who didn't cuss, didn't talk trash. He was a serious person. Very concerned about his mother."

"Why?"

"'Cause she was working herself into an early grave. Jeez, Josiah, you're getting my feathers ruffled."

"I know these are irritating questions, but they've got to be asked," I replied calmly. "Here's the last one. I heard a rumor that Sarah was having financial problems, but she tells me everything was fine."

"I think she's doing okay. If she was having money trouble, she didn't tell Irene or me. We sure would have helped her out."

I motioned for Jefferson Davis to pull me out of the chair. He obliged and stood me on my wobbly legs.

"I hope you can put this to rest for Irene's sake. She hasn't had a decent night's sleep since Jamie died."

"She says his spirit is restless."

"Second sight runs in her people, but I wish she'd let this go. It's upsetting."

I gave Jeff a hug. "I will do what I can."

He gave me several bundles of day lilies and waved off the money I offered. I happily inhaled their mild fragrance. I noticed several city honeybees trying to gather pollen from Irene's flowers. There must be a hive nearby as bees have a territory of two miles, but they like to stay close to home if they can. The thought that someone might have a hive on their rooftop was pleasing.

On the way back I ran into Morgan Mayfield, the owner of Sawyier's Vineyard.

"Hey, baby cakes," he said teasingly. "Folks said you looked like Quasimodo, but you look decent for an old gal who's been banged up a bit."

"I look damn smashing, Morgan," I rejoined.

"And that is after being smashed," countered Morgan.

I lifted my hair to show him my surgical scars. Then I lifted my dress to show him the huge scar that ran up my left leg. Pulling the hearing aid off, I let Morgan try it on.

"That's nothing," bragged Morgan, handing back the hearing aid. "Look at this. Tractor turned over on me." He rolled up his shirtsleeve and showed me a nasty jagged scar that ran the length of his forearm. "And look at this," he pulled up his shirttail, revealing a surgery scar on his lower abdomen. "Appendicitis. I've got another one but I'd have to pull off my pants to show you."

"Oh, please do," I teased. "Got any tattoos?"

"I'll show you my tattoos, if you show me yours," he grinned good-naturedly.

"I'll have to get some first. Hey Morgan, I've got something serious to ask. You know anything about Sarah Dunne or the Silver Creek Vineyard?"

Morgan scratched his head. "They make good wine. All the grapes are Kentucky grown grapes, not grape juice imported in from California. I can't stand it when local wineries do that. Sarah makes a merlot that I think is first class."

"So Silver Creek has a good reputation."

"I haven't heard anything negative about them. Sarah is known for being honest, paying her bills on time. No fights with other wineries."

"Not even the Golden Sun Vineyard?"

"That stuff about the first commercial winery is just business. It's not personal. I heard Peterson is going out of his way to help Sarah with that river tour he's having this summer. Wish I had thought of that. Great idea."

"Well, enough about them. How are you doing?"

"Life couldn't be better, Josiah. I'm proud of the wines we are making. Here – let me get you some before you take off."

"I can't do that."

"Yes, you can. Don't be so bossy, Miss Hossy." He handed me several bottles of Sawyier's Cabernet Sauvignon and Riesling wines. Giving me a big hug,

Morgan invited me to hear him sing next week at the winery before he returned to his booth to help pack up the few bottles of wine left.

Returning to my own booth site, I found Jake packing the car. "How much money did I make?" I asked Jake.

"You made the sum total of $624.00."

Pursing my lips while making a mental calculation of the bills I needed to pay, I replied, "Not too shabby for the first Saturday back, but it won't make me rich. Sales are going to have to pick up if I am going to be solvent this year." I scratched my neck. "Well, I'll think about that tomorrow." I sat in my chair and watched Jake finish packing up the Prius, which was not an ideal car for this kind of work. I pined for my rusted, beat-up van, which now took up space in one of the barns. After Jake got me settled in the car, I figured I had enough energy for a meal, so I directed Jake to Ted's house.

We had a delightful lunch and spirited conversation about politics. Ted's wife loved Jake, even though they came from opposite ends of the political spectrum with Jake surprisingly being very conservative. While his politics were not to my taste, I was proud of the way he debated Ted's wife point by point as she was well known for being very informed on current events and Washington shenanigans. But before I became too exhausted, Jake gave them our thank yous and goodbyes.

On the way out, the wife gave me two biographies on Kentucky women she had finished reading – Laura Clay and Jenny Wiley. I loved reading biographies, so I was pleased and discontented at the same time. There was no point in telling her I had trouble seeing print now unless it was large. I was hesitant in telling people what was busted. It tended to make them queasy. Perhaps I could talk Franklin into reading them to me.

But she was not happy when Jake deposited a box full of books regarding Franz Kafka on her living room floor. "Why would you get someone fourteen books on Kafka?" she asked her husband. "What kind of a joke is that to play on someone who is sick?"

"I thought it was amusing," Ted replied, "but I can see now that I was wrong." His shoulders slumped in defeat but when she turned her head, he winked at me. Ted had the marital policy that he could be right or he could be happy.

On the way home, I pointed out interesting older homes, regaling Jake with their significance. He liked hearing about the local history, or at least he pretended to enjoy it.

We turned into the driveway. It wasn't until we saw the flashing lights of the police cars surrounding the tobacco barn that we knew there had been trouble. I saw Detective Goetz leaning against a car writing in his notebook.

Jake parked the car and jumped out.

I followed suit.

Spying Shaneika sitting on a bale of hay, I went over to her.

"What's wrong? What's happened?"

Sobbing into a towel, she could only point to the barn.

"Not Comanche!" I sputtered. Spinning around, I attempted to make my way inside the barn.

Detective Goetz blocked my way. "You don't want to see this, Josiah. Take my word."

"Get out of my way," I demanded.

He reluctantly stepped aside.

I walked into a storm of commotion.

Comanche was hysterical in his stall, but alive. Neighing, Comanche kicked and bucked while several hands from Lady Elsmere's farm tried to calm him so they could lead him out.

I looked about, wondering what was making the stallion so crazy. Then I saw it. "Oh, merciful God," I whispered.

Someone had taken one of Comanche's companion goats, slit her throat and hung her upside down near the horse's stall. Blood was streaked on the walls as though it had been collected and thrown.

Feeling my knees start to buckle, I cried out.

Goetz, who had followed, caught me. "Sit here," he advised, placing me gently on a bale of hay. "That's a pretty awful sight."

I could now smell the blood staining the ground. There were splashes of blood on the stalls, on the horse's equipment, on the hay bales. "Who could do such a thing?" I asked, tears threatening to spill.

Goetz handed me his handkerchief. "You need to ask? People are shits. That's all."

"Do you think it's O'nan?"

"That's what we're working on. But Ms. Todd has made plenty of enemies on her own. Could be anyone." He pulled up a clean bale of hay next to me. "I need to ask you some questions." He waited until I nodded. "Where have you been today?"

I had to think for a minute. My thoughts were rattled. "I was at the Farmers' Market. Just got home."

"What time did you leave the farm?"

"Jake and I left the house at five this morning."

Goetz wrote that down in his worn tattered notebook. "Did you notice anything unusual?"

"The farm was quiet. We would have heard Comanche if the goat had been killed at that time." I grabbed his sleeve. "We had problems with bees last week. Someone ran over some of my bees."

"Matt has already informed me." Goetz grew quiet as Shaneika's vet strode past us. We watched him finally calm the grieving horse and slowly lead him outside to a waiting van.

Everyone froze as the distraught Thoroughbred trotted by. The surviving nanny goat followed. There was blood smeared on her back.

Her companion still hung from the rafters by its hooves. Even from where I was sitting there were welts and cuts on the dead goat, confirming that the animal had been tortured before its throat was slit. I smelled singed hair. "Was that animal burned?" I asked, hoping Goetz would say no.

"Looks like a cigarette."

"Please cut that pitiful animal down," I requested.

"We need to do some more work in here. Let's get you out of here," Goetz said, pulling me to my feet. "I want you to know that this is being given high priority." We walked outside together.

Matt and Jake were huddled around Shaneika.

I went over to her. "I'm so sorry."

The vet closed the gate on the horse van with a sharp clanging. Shaneika gave the driver a signal and the van turned around. "I am going to board Comanche at another farm. Don't know if I'm coming back," she said curtly.

Before I could respond, she rose and hopped into the van as it was making its way down the gravel road.

Matt, Jake and I stared stupidly at each other.

It was finally Jake who came to action in the guilty silence. "Matt, I think you better come to the big house. I need to deposit Boss Lady there. Then you and I need to search the farm with the police. We know where to look."

"Sure thing," agreed Matt. He followed us to the Butterfly in his car.

Jake did a quick search of the house, noting that Baby was asleep in his bed. He brought in the food purchased from the Farmers' Market and asked me to put it up. Then he and Matt left, each with a walkie-talkie and a stun baton. Jake took his gun off safety.

I put the food up as requested and then wandered into my bedroom with the walkie-talkie clutched in my hand.

Baby was still asleep. "Hey Baby," I said. "Could use your company now." He didn't respond. I poked him with my toe. No response.

"That's odd," I muttered. I gave Baby a harder shove with my foot. No response again. I shrugged. He was really taking a snooze.

Opening the closet door, I checked on the kittens. The barn cat and her babies were sleeping soundly. The mother cat opened her eyes for a moment and then returned to slumber land as I filled her food bowl.

"You were right to come," I told her. "You're safe here." She yawned in response to my prattle. Closing the closet door, I sat in the vanity chair taking off my shoes and the special hose I wore on my left leg. I was tugging on the hose when I noticed something funny about the Haitian paintings, but couldn't discern what. I kept staring until finally realizing what it was.

A sudden spike of fear caused me to tremble and I could barely make myself turn around to glance down the hallway. Seeing no one there, I lunged for the bedroom door and breathed a sigh of relief when the sound of the lock snapped into place. Grabbing the walkie-talkie on the vanity, I pressed the talk button. While peeking outside my patio door, I whispered, "Jake. Matt. Get back here quick and bring that vet with you. Baby's been drugged!"

Forty-five minutes later, the vet left the house and Baby was drowsily drinking out of my toilet bowl.

I sat on the vanity chair.

Jake sat on my bed, looking glum. "I didn't see today coming. After the bees, I should have, but escalations of this type are not so fast and furious." He rubbed his chin. "I should have seen it coming."

"None of us did."

"I'm the professional. I am supposed to notice patterns. This is way out of hand." Jake shook his head. "What made you suspect Baby was drugged?"

"The paintings on the wall," I pointed.

Matt stood in the doorway with a tray of iced tea.

I greedily accepted a glass.

Matt stared at the wall and pointed. "They've been switched. I should know as I helped Josiah put them up."

"He must have drugged Baby's outdoor water bowl or thrown a piece of drugged meat onto the property this morning when Baby was out doing his business. It's the only way he could have gotten past this mastiff in the house. He sure wanted to leave you a message," spoke Jake.

"And what's the message?" I asked.

Jake's left eye twitched just a tad before answering. "That he can get to you any time in your own home."

"Why not kill Baby like the goat?"

"Maybe the perp just ran out of time?" suggested Matt, running his hand through his dark hair. "Because the Saturday tour was due. And the tour doesn't go in the barn, but drives past it in a bus. They wouldn't have heard the horse throwing a ruckus."

"Shaneika puts Comanche in the barn every night either by herself or she gets someone from Lady Elsmere's farm, but the help always lets the horse out in the morning because Shaneika is in town for work . . ."

"Except on the weekends, when she drives out here," interjected Jake.

"Why was Comanche still in the barn?" I asked.

"Shaneika overslept and came out later," answered Matt. "She found Comanche hysterical."

"Someone would have to have known our routines to escape detection. Are you sure the hermit is not responsible for this?" I asked.

"I really doubt it. We did a psychological profile on him plus none of his tests showed any biological reason for this type of aggressive behavior. This was the work of someone who can maneuver undetected and work fast. This was not sloppy. It was calculated to bring the maximum amount of fear. That is what this is all about."

"Well, he did a good job because I'm scared," remarked Matt.

"I'm mad," I snorted. "That poor goat was the sweetest animal. She deserved better."

"I've called a locksmith to change all your locks this afternoon," stated Jake. "But who has keys to the house?"

I tried to think. It wasn't easy as my brain felt addled. "Ummmh, Matt and Shaneika have a key. You. And Lady Elsmere, in case I lose my key."

"Where does she keep the key?" asked Jake.

"Charles keeps it in a kitchen drawer."

"Anyone else?"

I shook my head.

"Charles got a beef with you?" Jake asked.

"Heavens no. Charles would never do anything like this nor anyone in his family. Only a very few people know this, but when Lady Elsmere dies, Charles gets the house with an endowment. It is not in his interest to stir up trouble."

"You've got to be kidding," Matt said. "Charles gets the farm?"

"He gets the farm, house and an eight million dollar endowment for upkeep on the farm as long as the property is kept intact. If Charles dies, it goes to his daughters. The rest of June's money goes to various charities in the Bluegrass. Charles and a senior member of her bank will manage her philanthropic money, and both will get substantial management fees."

"How did he arrange that sweet deal?" asked Jake, looking amused. He glanced at Matt who shook his head in disbelief.

"I talked June into it," I replied smugly.

"You?"

"June was always talking about how she wants to leave the Earth a better place. I challenged her to put her money where her mouth was. I made a case that Charles, who is a descendant of Henry Clay's Dupuy family, deserved the estate as he had served her faithfully and competently, and because of his illustrious background. After all, the Dupuys are historical aristocracy 'round these parts. Until then, she was just going to leave

Charles a few measly hundred thousand dollars, and give the farm to a worthless Yankee great-nephew of hers from Ohio, who would have chopped the farm up into a subdivision. So I talked her into switching bequests." I sipped my tea as the two men stared at me. "Charles knows this and will do anything for me . . . well, just about. I don't think he'd kill for me. Anyway the Dupuy family deserved this inheritance."

"Maybe it's this nephew who caused today's troubles," wondered Jake.

"Nope, he died from alcohol poisoning last year and left no heirs."

Matt scratched his forehead and brushed back his thick hair. "Let's start from the beginning of this wild little tale. Who are the Dupuys and why is Charles important because he is a Dupuy?"

I gave Matt a pitying look. People should know their history. Really, they should. "Charles' ancestors were Aaron and Charlotte Dupuy, who were the house servants of Henry Clay. You know who Henry Clay is, don't you?"

"Get on with it," demanded Matt.

"These two families were tightly bound by history. In the early 1800s, Clay's estate, Ashland, encompassed six hundred acres and over fifty slaves, some of whom were the Dupuy family. Aaron Dupuy was Clay's personal man while Charlotte, his wife, took care of the Clay children. Henry Clay even took them to Washington with him while he served as Secretary of State. It is there that Charlotte Dupuy legally sued Henry Clay for her freedom. He left her there while he took Aaron and her children back to Kentucky when his term was up.

"You've got to understand the times. This was a big, big legal battle between the two families. It was national news and made headlines.

"If Charlotte won her case, then slaves would be able to take legal action against their masters. It would have turned the South upside down."

"What happened?" inquired Matt.

"Charlotte lost her case and was returned as Henry Clay's property. But later on, Clay does emancipate Charlotte and one daughter. He must have freed the rest of the family too. Later census records list Aaron and Charlotte as freed slaves. But Henry Clay's death shows you how intertwined these two families were. It was Aaron who drove Henry Clay's funeral carriage to the Lexington Cemetery in 1852. I doubt he would have done that if he had not had some deep emotion for Clay."

Jake tapped his foot. "So what?"

"Charles is a direct descendant. His family helped build Lexington. They should get more than just the leavings. That's why I argued on his behalf."

"Isn't June's dinner party tonight?" interjected Jake.

"Yes, but I have declined."

"Undecline. We need to go and find out stuff. Someone from Lady Elsmere's farm could have easily come back and forth without detection."

"Someone could have picked the lock," said Matt.

Jake shook his head. "That's harder than it looks. It's not always easy like you see on TV. I don't think our guy could have risked taking the time. The tour was coming and he also had to watch out for you, Matt. You were home, after all."

"Was that a shot?" asked Matt, his hackles rising.

I interceded. "The key from June's house is the only logical explanation and Charles will help us. He sits on the Animal Humane Society's board. Besides this happening to me, which will piss Charles off, he dislikes cruelty to animals. Okay? I'm going to call Charles right now and meet him at the gate." I picked up the phone and dialed. I looked at Jake's and Matt's confused faces. "That's where I meet Charles when we talk privately – the property gate. If somebody at June's house used that spare key, Charles will know who."

"That doesn't explain how he knew the code for the security system," said Jake.

"I gave the code to Charles' daughters so they could get into the house for the tours," said Matt, "but they were to keep it a secret."

"I also gave them a briefing on security for the house," rejoined Jake, looking irritated.

"Charles probably has the code number written somewhere near the key," I said. "The key is no good without the security code."

"Christ," muttered Jake. "There are just too many people coming and going out of this house with too much information," he said looking hard at Matt.

"I guess that is directed at me," replied Matt. "She's got to make a living and this house is one of the few ways Josiah can make money in her present condition. It's not like she is well enough to go outside the home and work. The tours stay as they are. If you are as good as you claim to be, you can work around this."

"I might have been able to if I had been informed that practically everyone in this county had access to the security codes," growled Jake, his voice growing louder with each word. He was upset and wanted to take his anger out on someone.

Not wishing for a full-blown argument, I spoke up. "I need to meet with Charles. Can I go now? I don't think you need me for anything else. Do you, Jake? Matt?" I tried to look very innocent and vulnerable.

Although still shook up, I talked Jake into letting me go alone.

The cops were still at the barn. He and Matt needed to join the search party going about the farm. Jake reluctantly agreed.

Charles was already waiting when I arrived. We chatted for twenty minutes until I was satisfied with the new information he gave me. We hatched a plan that was doable. If I were right, it still would be dangerous, even with all the safeguards implemented.

"See you around eight tonight," I said to Charles. We shook hands and parted.

On the way to the Butterfly, I checked my bee yards. On the hive cover where I had left the honey was a stick with a piece of blue cloth hanging from it. Underneath was a note written on the back of the one I had written to Moshe Goren. "Mrs. Reynolds, I did not harm your bees or your farm animals. It is not the Jewish way to mistreat dumb creatures. Mr. Moshe Goren."

I put the note in my pocket and left with an uneasy feeling in my gut. It was going to be a very long night.

# 17

I was wearing an off-the-shoulder blue Dior which I hadn't been able to get into for close to nine years. My hair was upswept, sparkling with rhinestone pins I had purchased at the mall along with the blue satin bathroom slippers on my swollen feet. I joined Matt, who was playing solitaire in the great room. Franklin was sullenly making popcorn in the kitchen. They were going to baby-sit a still woozy Baby and the kittens. Matt looked nervous.

Placing my hand on his, I gave him my best smile. "It will be okay," I whispered. I knew we both were thinking of the last time I went to Lady Elsmere's home for dinner.

Franklin plopped the bowl down on the table, spilling the popcorn everywhere, including my lap.

"Franklin, you'd better not have gotten butter on this chiffon."

"I'm so miserable that I am not going. I miss out on everything."

"Be glad you missed out on this afternoon," admonished Matt. "It was pretty horrible."

Franklin stared out the window. Every so often, he would let out a long sigh.

"Franklin, if you promise to quit sighing, I'll give a dinner party and ask Lady Elsmere over here. That way she can meet you and she will return the invitation . . . if she likes you. Will that make you happy?"

"A proper dinner party?"

"Well, a little more casual than hers, but yes, a proper dinner party."

"What's this about a dinner party?" asked Jake, coming out of his room in a tuxedo.

My heart did a little flutter. Jake looked very handsome. I must be crazy for men in formal attire.

"Thanks, Matt, for the loan of the penguin suit," said Jake.

"Looks good on you," affirmed Matt. "And you look very pretty tonight, Josiah. Very pretty, indeed."

Jake's ruddy skin gleamed above the white collar while his thick black hair sparkled blue-black under the lighting. "Can you tell I'm wearing a gun?"

"NO!" Matt and I chorused.

"I can tell he's packin'," quipped Franklin.

Jake smoothed the jacket, took a deep breath and said, "Let's get this show on the road."

After hearing a knock at the door, Franklin ran to see if Lady Elsmere had sent the Bentley. She had.

Jake held out his hand, pulling me out of my chair.

Franklin handed me my sleek ebony walking stick with the silver head of a wolf that he had purchased in Key West.

Jake and I walked out of the Butterfly in style.

I hoped no one could tell my stomach was doing somersaults. I was nervous.

We arrived without mishap.

Lady Elsmere was waiting for us on the portico. Her frail body dripped heavily with diamonds. I don't know how her bony skeleton supported the weight. And, of course, one of her three tiaras was perched on her coiffed head like a neon motel beacon.

Charles was standing behind her as always. He winked at us.

"Daaarling, I was aghast when I heard about what happened at your place today. I didn't know if you would come tonight or not. And that would have simply screwed with my table arrangement."

I kissed her wrinkled cheek. "Thanks for being so supportive, June." I turned to Jake. "May I introduce Jacob Dosh to you, my nephew from Oklahoma. We call him Jake. Jake, this is Lady Elsmere."

"How do you do," he said, giving a little bow.

She peered closer at him. "I thought you were going to bring the divine Matthew Garth with you."

"He was detained, but Jake can eat with a fork and a knife if dinner calls for it."

"Do you flirt, young man?"

"No ma'am."

"Well, that's discouraging," she stated as she swept inside the house.

Charles shook his head, muttering the word "contrary."

We followed suit and found ourselves in the library, just like last year. I heard June say before I stepped in, "Here she is." I entered to see the same guests as the year before . . . standing in attention. They clapped upon seeing me.

I turned to June. "Let me guess. I'm the guest of honor."

June reached over and hugged me. "I just wanted to do something nice for you. I thought if I could re-create that night again and nothing bad happened when you went home, it would help. Then that awful event at the barn this morning. I guess my dinners are jinxed for you." She looked downcast.

Out of the corner of my mouth, I said, "I've been telling you that for years." I stepped forward. "Thank you all for coming. Thank you, Lady Elsmere, for honoring me. It has been a long . . . nine months now, yes, I think that is correct, but I am delighted to be here tonight. If I don't immediately respond to the conversation, please excuse me. The conk on the head I received sometimes makes my response time slower."

There was a ripple of nervous laughter. I placed my hand on Jake's arm. "Stand your ground and show no fear," I whispered.

Reverend Humble and his wife, Ruth, stepped up to greet me. They pumped my hand feverishly as I thanked them for coming. They looked suspiciously at Jake as though trying to place him on the people yardstick when I introduced him.

"Hello, Larry," I said to retired Special Agent Larry Bingham. "Long time no see. Hello, Brenda."

"I can't believe how well you look, Josiah," breathed Brenda, holding my hands. Hers were cold. She cocked her head at Jake. "Is this the young man who was with you last year?"

"No, that was Matthew Garth. This is Jake Dosh, my nephew recently out of Oklahoma."

"Oh," she said with a disappointed lilt to her voice, but then she caught herself and gave Jake a big smile. "Happy to meet you, Mr. Dosh."

"I thought you'd still be drinking dinner out of a straw," said Larry, pushing his wife a little to the side.

She gave him an apologetic glance before moving toward June.

"Sorry to disappoint you. Larry, this is my nephew, Jake."

Larry gave Jake a quick once-over. "Well, if you say so." He leaned in toward Jake, "Big piece you're carrying. Must be a semi-automatic."

Jake's eyes narrowed but he said nothing. He gave Larry the once-over.

Meriah Caldwell, the famous mystery writer, stepped forward. "Nice to see you again."

"How's your new book coming along?" I tapped my temple. "See, I remembered."

"Almost finished. We can discuss it over dinner."

"Look forward to it," I said smiling, but was inwardly groaning. I made a mental bargain that I'd refrain from boring the party with tales of my ill health if Meriah refrained from boring us with details of her novel. And we'd all just have to hope no one had any grandchildren.

"Dinner is served, Madam," announced Charles, coming to my rescue.

That was good news, as my legs were giving out. Jake escorted me into the dining room, where June had laid out her best china and antique English silverware. In the center of the table was placed a stunning floral arrangement. I was pleased to see the flowers were Irene's starburst lilies.

"Most of everything tonight was purchased at the Farmers' Market," announced Lady Elsmere proudly. "I knew you would enjoy that." She gave my hand a tender squeeze. "I can't believe how good you look." She looked quizzically at my head. "What's that thing on your ear?"

I took off my hearing aid to show everyone. "It's one of those high-tech ones. They're supposed to be barely detectable, but it seems everyone detects them right off. Go figure."

Meriah Caldwell inspected it for a time before handing it back. "Incredibly sleek."

"Yes, considering they have a GPS built into them," stated Larry. "These little doodads have military applications."

Meriah lit up. "That's very interesting." She started to say something and then thought better of it.

"Yes, isn't it," I replied sullenly, watching with displeasure as the servers placed bowls of vichyssoise before us. This was the first time I had heard of a GPS device in my hearing aid. Now I knew why everyone noticed it.

Two of the servers were Charles' grandsons while the third was a newcomer to Lady Elsmere's staff, whom Charles had told me about this afternoon.

Jake watched the newcomer from under his lids.

"Mr. Dosh, from your accent . . . you're not from around here," stated Lady Elsmere.

"No ma'am. I'm from Oklahoma like Mrs. Reynolds told you."

"That's a Southerner's polite way of asking who your people are," said Brenda.

Lady Elsmere continued undeterred, "You say that you are Josiah's nephew. But our little Jo doesn't have any siblings. She's an only child."

"Well, she does in fact . . . but from the wrong side of the blanket." Jake gave Lady Elsmere a wicked grin.

She had the good grace to turn red.

"Oh, do go on," popped up Brenda. "Sounds juicy."

"If I have more champagne, I just might tell you the story of my ill-fated parents," teased Jake.

I cut in. "Lady Elsmere, did I tell you that my daughter is working on a case where a Botticelli was stolen from a private home in Amsterdam?"

Oh, what whoppers Jake and I were telling tonight. I had no idea what art case she was working on, if any. I just hoped my nose wasn't growing longer. I stole a glance at Jake's.

"Speaking of the prodigal daughter, when is she coming home? I haven't seen her since last October when she whisked you off to Key West. Why Key West? I mean, who goes to Key West anymore. Since Tennessee Williams died and the island built those horrible condos, who cares."

"Because the island is small enough to be contained and has a good police force," muttered Larry.

"Contained for what?" asked Meriah.

"Security, I would think," piped Brenda.

Larry gave an almost imperceptible shake of his head. Brenda quickly asked for the rolls.

I picked up the trail of Lady Elsmere's question. "I expect her home within the month," I said.

"It was amazing how she pulled herself up after those congressional hearings several years back," commented Meriah.

My voice was heated. "That was a dog and pony show."

Jake intervened. "Josiah tells me that you like to base your dinners on famous ones from the past. Can you explain tonight's conception?"

Lady Elsmere beamed. "Thank you, but we are just having Josiah's favorites tonight. Prime rib, potatoes au gratin, asparagus, fresh yeast rolls and crème brulee for dessert."

"Why did we start off with vichyssoise?" I asked. "I don't care for cold potato soup."

Lady Elsmere snorted. "Because I like it and detest the rest of the swill I am obliged to eat tonight."

Larry speared a big piece of juicy prime rib with his fork. "Some swill."

"Basically peasant food," twittered Lady Elsmere. "No real finesse in the cooking. Just don't burn the meat."

"Yes, but happy peasants," I said, happily pouring au jus on my prime rib. I had to cut it into very tiny pieces in order to chew. I didn't mind, but Charles, seeing that I was having trouble with the knife, brought me a new plate with the prime rib already cut along with the vegetables.

"Madame, your meat looks overcooked. Let me refresh your plate," Charles said as he switched dishes.

It spared me further embarrassment as the other guests were watching me struggle with the knife.

Ruth Humble said, "Well, dinner is delicious as always."

"Yes, it is," concurred Reverend Humble. "Tonight is a special treat. I must admit that those French sauces and pickled vegetables of past meals have upset my stomach."

Ruth looked with alarm between her husband and Lady Elsmere, aka June Webster from Monkey's Eyebrow, Kentucky.

A dark cloud gathered over Lady Elsmere's face, but she remained quiet.

I knew, though, that Reverend and Mrs. Humble had just been written off the guest list.

So did Ruth. She gave her twit of a husband a curdling look.

We chatted about inane subjects until we retired to the library again for dessert and coffee.

Jake nodded at me, giving me the signal.

I excused myself to use the powder room, but headed to the kitchen where I encountered a skeleton crew of workers.

The cook and her people had left, leaving the cleaning up to Charles' staff, which comprised Charles' grandsons and a new employee who had been on board for a month.

I went up to the new staff member who was carefully washing the antique china by hand. "Hello," I said cheerfully. "My name is Mrs. Reynolds. I was wondering if I could get a glass of milk. My stomach is in an uproar."

The young man looked at his fellow workers, who suddenly had become very busy with other tasks. "Sure thing," he said, slowly strutting to the refrigerator.

I studied him while he poured the milk. His features were pleasant enough but he was very thin, as though he hadn't eaten much protein as a child. His nails were filed and clean but looked yellowish. His blond hair was thin and laid limply across a low sloping shiny forehead. At the back of the neck, one could see the tip of a tattoo. His face was scarred from acne, but what really interested me were pinpoints of swelling on his neck, face and hands.

Handing me the glass, he watched me drink it. I didn't like the expression on his face. It was a smirk – like he had one over me.

"I'm dying for a smoke. Can I bum a cigarette off you?"

"How did you know that I smoked?" he asked, reaching for a pack in his shirt pocket.

"I saw the nicotine stains on your fingers," I said. "Dead giveaway."

One of Charles' grandsons spoke up. "Miss Josiah, you know you're not supposed to smoke with your asthma. You give that cigarette back or I'm going to call Mr. Garth."

I made a face at him. "I can't do anything anymore without someone telling on me." Handing the new guy my empty glass, I asked, "Mind if I have another? At least I can have that."

He shrugged, "You're the guest," and gave me another which I drank sitting on a stool.

"You must be new to Lady Elsmere's staff. I don't think I've seen you before."

His face registered nothing, but he shifted his weight. "I've been on board for over a month."

"I hope you like it here."

"Yes, very much, thank you." He reached for the empty glass.

"Oh my goodness!" I exclaimed, pointing to the swollen wounds on his hands. "Those look like bee stings. And you've got some on your neck too. My bees didn't do that, did they?"

He jerked his hands away. "No ma'am. I was cleaning out an old shed and a nest of wasps got me. Had nothing to do with your bees."

"That's good, because that's an awful lot of stings. I don't want to get sued." We both chuckled. "Well, I'd best be getting back."

His brown eyes regarded me suspiciously as he helped me off the stool. I headed toward the library again, where I met Charles in the hallway. I nodded as I passed.

Returning to my seat in the library, I waited fifteen minutes before I announced I was weary and needed to leave.

The men stood as I struggled to get out of my chair. Finally, Jake pulled me onto my feet.

Everyone seemed relieved to see me go.

I still wasn't all that steady on my feet and that tended to make people nervous. I was too blasé to think that it was out of concern for me personally.

Meriah Caldwell escorted me to the front door. "I have never gotten to use my invitation to see the Butterfly."

I was tempted to say that tours were every Tuesday and Saturday. Jake and I needed to get away fast. "Are you staying . . . again?"

"Yes. I'll be a guest of June's for some time. I am finishing up my book about murder in the Bluegrass and need to soak up more ambience . . ."

"Ah, gee, that's great," I cut in. "Well . . . please excuse me. It's been a long day."

"We never did discuss my book at dinner."

"Another time, please. I'm starting to ache all over. I am afraid that I sat too long. Cramps up my muscles."

"Of course," she said.

Jake bade Meriah goodnight and got us both into the Bentley.

She stood on the portico waving as Charles drove Jake and me down the driveway.

Safely ensconced in the car, I asked, "Charles?"

"It's done."

"How did you get him?"

Jake interrupted. "Don't tell her a thing, Charles. Everyone needs plausible deniability. In fact, let me out right here."

Charles stopped the car and turned toward Jake. "I can drive back to the shed."

"No," said Jake emphatically. "If for some reason we got the wrong guy, both of you can say truthfully under a lie detector test that you let me out here so I could stretch my legs on a walk home. Remember, plausible deniability." He placed a hand on Charles' shoulder. "Just drop off Mrs. Reynolds like you would usually do. She'll be okay. Matt and Franklin are there. I talked with them just before I got into the car. Now, I need to walk to stretch my legs. I'll see you, Boss Lady, at the house."

"Okay," I said, looking straight ahead. I knew I was not to see Jake disappear into the woods and reenter June's property. As soon as I heard the car door shut, I said, "Let's go, Charles."

"I hope this works," muttered Charles, "or all our fannies will be in hot water."

# 18

The next morning I was awakened by the doorbell ringing. Putting on a robe, I went to the front door, checked the security monitor and, taking a deep breath, pressed the button that unlocked the alcove door. I opened the front steel door and waited. "Good morning, Detective Goetz."

"Morning. May I come in?" Goetz asked. He followed me into the great room. I motioned for him to sit. "You were still asleep?"

"I had a late night at June's . . . I mean Lady Elsmere's last night."

He took out his notebook and thumbed through it. "Dinner ended about ten o'clock."

"That's late for me anymore. I don't have the stamina to stay up. Why do you care?"

"Just trying to get a picture of last night's events." Goetz licked the end of his pencil. He looked around. "Where's your boy?"

"My boy?" I repeated in confusion. "Oh, you mean Jake. He's either in his bedroom, doing a security walk or swimming laps in the pool. I know he is up because the coffee is on. Would you like some?"

"That would be nice."

I limped over to the kitchen and poured two mugs of coffee. I brought them back on a tray with sugar, honey and milk. My hands shook a little bit, but I could put that down to my condition. I twitched all the time anyway.

Goetz grabbed the tray and put it on the coffee table. "Thanks," he said, picking up a mug.

"What's going on?" I asked. "Did you find out who hurt my animals?"

"Got a call from the hospital last night that Charles had brought in an employee who was having a very bad trip – jacked out on who knows how many drugs. The docs called the police 'cause he was ranting about being abducted from Lady Elsmere's kitchen and shot up with drugs while being interrogated."

"What employee?" I asked. "Was he serving dinner last night? I saw the serving staff and they looked fine. How absurd."

"That's what the cop who took the report thought, but he passed the report on to me 'cause he knew I had an interest what in goes on here." Goetz scratched his ear.

"The thing that got my attention was that in the list of drugs in this guy's system was scopolamine. Do you know what that is?"

I shook my head.

"It's actually used in small dosages for motion sickness but also used for military interrogation. Of course, it's illegal to use this drug like that, but used it is. It's a truth serum. Very powerful and very dangerous. I said to myself – who would have something like this in their medicine chest? I said to myself – doesn't Josiah's daughter have military connections?"

I interrupted, "Did you do a background check on this guy?"

Goetz reared back in his seat. He paused for a long moment, looking at me.

I stared back.

Finally he said, "Yes, I did." He looked at his notes. "His real name is George Fanning. A two-time loser from Tennessee. Has numerous minor convictions for assault and petty thievery. Loves cockfights and has been known to bet on dogfights as well. Has served two terms at West Tennessee State Penitentiary for robbery with a deadly weapon." He took a sip of coffee. "This is where the story gets interesting. Charles hired this guy on a recommendation from a buddy of his from the VFW hall – a buddy that we can't find now. The employee gave his name as George Frank. Charles did a background check and gave him a drug test. The guy comes up clean, so Charles hires him. Been working for Lady Elsmere for about a month.

"Last night, Charles claims this guy comes at him out of nowhere and tries to attack him. Charles' grandkids pull this George Frank off and call the cops. The arresting officer calls an ambulance because this guy is foaming at the mouth – literally. On the way to the hospital he begins making these wild claims that he was abducted and taken to an old shed on Lady Elsmere's property where he was interrogated and given drugs by someone wearing a mask. But he recognizes the voice of the interrogator as being a guest at the dinner party. Your escort, ummm, or your bodyguard," Goetz said, looking at his notes. "Jake Dosh, the guy who was with you in Key West. The guy who was carrying a gun yesterday under his shirt at the barn. The guy who never lets you out his sight.

"Here's another twist to the story. This Fanning says that he never attacked Charles – that Charles is lying. Once the interrogation was over, Charles' boys came in and just took him back up to the main house and called the police, where all four lied to the cops about the attack."

"I don't care about what this George claims. Did he have anything to do with killing that goat or drugging Baby?"

Goetz took a deep breath. "I think so. We did a search this morning and found a knife in his apartment that tested positive for blood. The lab is checking to see if it is goat's blood. Also found some roofies that would cause a dog to sleep heavily if given enough. This George Fanning also had meth over the user amount, so he'll go down for that. Yep, this George is a bad boy, no matter how you look at it."

"If you can tie the knife to the goat, my question is why?"

"Among the many fabulous tales coming out of this guy's mouth is one that he was drinking in some redneck bar in Memphis when he was approached by some guy who told him he could make an easy three grand. All he had to do was come here and make a little trouble. His job was to terrify you for a short period of time and then leave the state. He was given a thousand to start and then when finished, this guy would meet him in Tennessee to give him the rest of the two thousand. Easy money."

"Did he say who this guy was?"

"No names were exchanged, but George described the guy."

"And?" I clasped my hands, waiting for the worst.

"I'm very sorry, Josiah. It sounds like O'nan, but lots of guys look like him, you know."

I took a deep breath. "Do you believe he could have survived that fall?"

"Off the record?"

"Yeah."

"No, but stranger things have happened." He closed his notebook. "I'm sorry. I know what you've been through. I know that I have been a part of that worry, but I'm gonna catch him. I swear that I will catch O'nan if he's alive."

"Not his buddy anymore?" I replied sarcastically.

"I was never his buddy," sputtered Goetz. His eyes looked moist and concerned. "I know you won't believe this, but I ran a lot of interference with O'nan on your behalf."

"You're right. I don't believe it."

Goetz sighed and then stood. "Tell your boy that I want to talk with him . . . soon."

"Will do."

"I'll see myself out."

As soon as I heard the click of the door, I went to the security monitor and moved the camera joystick so I could watch Goetz leave. "Did you hear all that?" I asked.

"Yes," replied Jake, stepping from the shadows. "It concurs with what I found out last night. Fanning was sent up here to put you off your game, cause disruption, nothing more. He was never to attack you personally."

"In other words, a cat and mouse game."

"It would seem so."

"I hope you hurt him. I know that sounds awful but I hope you did."

"I gave him a small taste of what it's like to be trussed up and tortured."

"Did he say the man who gave him the money was O'nan?"

"Really doesn't know. He was to meet this guy in Jellico for the last payment."

"That's only three hours from here."

"It is what it is. You have a serious stalker problem."

I turned and faced Jake. I could feel his warm breath on my face. "Well, I'm made of sterner stuff. If O'nan is alive, he won't break me." I placed my hand on his chest, feeling the heat of his dark skin under his shirt. "May God forgive me," I whispered, "but I hate O'nan. I can't forgive him. I pray, but there is no forgiveness in me. Just cold hate."

Jake moved closer. I could feel his lips next to my hair. He took a deep breath, smelling me. Lifting my face, I searched his. Jake started leaning toward me as though he might kiss me.

The telephone rang. As if awakened from a dream, Jake moved to answer the phone.

*Jumping Jehosaphat*, I thought. *Don't go out on a limb. Stay away from the hired help.*

"Yes ma'am. Affirmative. Thirteen hundred hours. Yes, ma'am. Affirmative." He hung up the phone.

"Was that my daughter?"

"She is sending a team to Memphis to pick up the trail."

"What is happening at one o'clock?"

"Cody is to arrive back here and she says that you are not to fire him again," grinned Jake.

"Can you take me into town?"

"Sure. What are you up to?"

"I want to buy some books." I passed Jake, deeply inhaling his scent, which reminded me of the sea. It made me giddy.  Uh oh.  I was in more than one kind of trouble.

\*

I opened the door to the Morris Book Shop on Southland Drive when I spotted Meriah Caldwell chatting with Bette Ann Gil, who was the director of a regional NPR radio station.  I turned to escape when I heard my name.  Swinging around, I gave them both a big smile.  "Meriah.  Bette Ann.  What an unexpected surprise."

"Hello, Josiah," said Bette Ann, leaning forward and giving me a kiss on the cheek.  Her expensive gold jewelry jangled as she leaned forward.  "Glad to see you again.  I was just telling Meriah that I had dinner with you last week and that your recovery was that of one who has visited Lourdes and seen a vision of the Holy Mother.  Miraculous.  But she tells me that she had dinner with you last night and there was another ruckus that involved the police.  My, but your life has taken such an interesting turn the past year, but enough about you.  Let's talk about me."

I gave them both a once-over.  "If I were Sherlock Holmes, I would be able to deduce that you two are up to something.  Are you two being naughty?"

Meriah started to speak, but Bette Ann placed a hand on Meriah's shoulder.  "Oh, please.  Let me tell her.  The fact is that we are indeed up to something.  Meriah wants her new book release party to take place here and I am going to use it as a fundraiser for the radio station. Meriah is going to give part of the proceeds from the sale of her books. We shall make money hand over fist." Bette Ann's eyes glittered. "And she wants you to be the guest of honor. And since you owe me several favors, I accepted for you . . . so you will be here."

Having parked the car, Jake entered. He looked surprised at seeing the three of us together, but moved quickly past us into the aisles of the store.

Meriah leaned her head toward Bette Ann. "That man was Josiah's escort last night at Lady Elsmere's house. She says he's her nephew." She gave Bette Ann a conspiratorial look.

"Really?" said Bette Ann. "What does the very handsome and dashing Matthew Garth say about this?"

"I think Matt is gay," said Meriah, her brow frowning. "Those are the vibes I got."

Gold bracelets flashed as Bette Ann pointed a manicured finger at me. "You told me that you were dating Matt when I asked you about him."

I shrugged. "Either way, he is unavailable . . . to you." Plopping down wearily in a chair, I had a sinking feeling that these two women were going to eviscerate me. "Meriah, what is your new book really about?"

Meriah opened her mouth, but Bette Ann interrupted her. "Oh, please. Let me tell her." Bette Ann sat next to me. "It takes place in Lexington during the '90s. It's about a young rich beautiful widowed horsewoman who is accused of murdering a competitor during the night before the Kentucky Derby. Of course, she didn't. But the psychopathic cop on the case doesn't believe her, so he tries to frame her. Anyway it goes on and on until the climax when they have this terrific row and she pushes him off a bridge into the Ohio River. Isn't that simply divine? I can't wait to read it." Bette Ann looked at me, beaming.

"Very original story, Meriah," I said, seething. "Too bad I'm going to get an injunction and stop the release of this book." I noticed that the employees of Morris Book Shop were busy with tasks near us so they could eavesdrop all the better.

Meriah, still standing, began to defend her book when Bette Ann held up her hand. "Oh please. Let me tell her. It's going to be a hit and you are going to be famous as well."

"Bette Ann, when did you start hating me so much?"

Bette Ann drew herself up. "Hate you? I am looking out for your interests. Now listen to me. I've heard through the grapevine that the city is going to settle and how much. It sounds like a lot, but my dear, let me be frank. In the end, it is not going to cover all your expenses, especially if you have to pay bodyguards." She made a gesture toward Jake. "And please don't insult my intelligence that he is your nephew. I mean really, Josiah, don't take me for a fool. He's got ex-Marine written all over him. Just look at the way he stands – like he's squeezing an orange between his butt cheeks. There are tight buns . . . but his are . . . well – incredible."

The three of us leaned over and checked out Jake's fanny.

"And, of course, that tattoo of Semper Fi seals it," Meriah said.

How Meriah knew that Jake had that tattoo stumped me. It could only be seen when he was swimming or otherwise undressed. Hmmm? The three of us turned again to admire Jake.

He looked up from his magazine and gave us a curious look when he caught the three of us staring.

Bette Ann swiveled her chair to get a better look. "Who is he really? What is he really? How much does he charge by the hour?"

"Don't be rude, Bette Ann," I admonished.

"Don't interrupt me. I'm on a roll," continued Bette Ann. "You need to write a book. I know you can't write about what happened to you according to the lawsuit stipulations, but it doesn't make any difference what kind of book you write. It can be that book on Kentucky art you always wanted to do. But if you wrote a Southern cookbook, it would sell like gangbusters around here. You would make a small fortune. And you need to have it finished when Meriah has the second of the trilogy released."

"Two more books about this horsewoman," I sputtered. "Hell's bells!"

"Well, you see," said Meriah nervously. "The cop doesn't die, but continues to harass our heroine from a distance, constantly putting her life in peril. I figure I can get at least three books out of this theme before the readers tire of it."

Bette Ann's eyes brightened. "I know! We can have a fundraising dinner at June's house celebrating your mystery and Josiah's new cookbook. Do you think she'd let us?"

"If it means getting her name in the paper, then I would say yes," I said.

"Then you'll do it. I can use the cookbook as a premium gift for my station's fundraiser. It will be great." Bette Ann clapped her hands together. "Please say yes, Josiah. I'll never say another rude thing to you again."

"Yes, you will," I laughed. "But I will give the cookbook some serious thought."

"I knew I could talk you into it," said Bette Ann smugly.

"Yes, yes, you've got the touch," Meriah said, pouting her lips. "Let's go. I'm late for my other appointment and you're driving." She pulled Bette Ann up from her chair. "Sorry to run," said Meriah, "but I've got to go." She gave an annoying look at Bette Ann. "Move it."

Bette Ann mouthed "call me" as she was being pushed out the door.

"I wonder where those two are going and what they're up to?" I said to myself.

Jake wandered over. "Get what you need and let's go. We've made ourselves very conspicuous." By that he meant I had made us conspicuous. It made his job harder. I could tell that the stress of being bodyguard, doctor, cook and bottle-washer was starting to get to Jake. He had asked my daughter for more help besides Cody, but she couldn't afford it. Jake was stuck.

I quickly picked out books on local wineries and a book with detailed maps of the Kentucky River.

Jake paid for them and hurried me out the door before I could talk with Wyn Morris, the owner.

For once I didn't argue. Jake had gone out on a limb for me and I was not going to repay him by being difficult. I knew what he was thinking. Was O'nan alive? Was he watching us now? Were the both of us going to get a bullet in the back? That would put anybody on edge.

O'nan was an excellent marksman. He had won many awards for his shooting ability. A headshot was not out of the question.

Maybe I should just go away on my own. I was endangering people's lives. Jake and Cody were paid to take risks, but not Franklin, Matt or Shaneika. Shaneika had already had the good sense to leave.

I knew I could talk Franklin into not coming around, but not Matt. Matt would stay with me through thick and thin, no matter what. Maybe when my daughter came home, she could talk Matt into leaving until this thing with O'nan was over. Matt could stay in town with Franklin.

I sank back into my car seat. I felt better. When my daughter came home, she would rework the scenario. She would get O'nan for me, if he had survived.

# 19

Regardless of what was going on in our personal lives, the animals needed tending to, and that also meant the bees. The nectar flow was so heavy I was afraid that the hives were becoming honey bound, which meant that the frames were filled with honey where the queen needed to lay eggs. It was tedious to go through the hives to switch out the nectar-filled frames or move them about in the hive. It took a long time and I couldn't handle the strain of working the hives anymore.

Jake absolutely refused to let me teach him. He wouldn't admit it but he was afraid of the bees and Matt simply didn't have the time anymore. So I had to call Larry and ask for help. And Larry, being the guy he was, came the next day.

I put on my bee veil over a sweatshirt and followed Larry into the different bee yards in my electric golf cart where I got as close as I could to the hives.

"You want me to kill the queen cells?" asked Larry, taking his hive tool to a peanut-sized queen cell.

"No. I never kill the young queens," I cautioned. "I just let nature take its course."

"Gonna cost you bees in swarming."

"That's why I've got swarm boxes all over the farm."

"Those things never work," scoffed Larry. He gently pulled out a frame heavy with brood and honey, bringing it over for my inspection. The queen was laying a good brood pattern. We both grunted our approval.

He pulled out another frame, which was nearly capped with beeswax. "Looks like you are going to have to harvest soon, Josiah," he said inspecting the hive body frame. "I bet there's three pounds of honey on this frame alone."

"Can you help me with the harvesting, Larry? I'll give you an eighth of my honey if you will."

"Skinflint. I'll take a third."

"No doing. Instead of robbing the hives, you're robbing me."

"Okay. Okay. A fourth of the total harvest."

"Done."

Larry got in the golf cart and pulled off his bee veil fishing for something to drink, while I drove over to Lady Elsmere's farm where I kept more hives. I parked on a small ridge overlooking her estate so we could admire her antebellum house and Thoroughbred mares with their colts munching contently on the bluegrass.

"Those look like Standards over there," remarked Larry.

"June is getting into show horses now as well."

He whistled. "She must have shitloads of money."

"She lost a lot when the stock market went south. I think she's only worth about twenty-five million now and most of that is tied up in property."

"Ahhh, I feel sorry for June," grinned Larry, bringing up a water bottle to his mouth. "Just a couple of mill in the old checking account?"

"Larry, have you heard anything in the spook gossip world about what happened here?"

He sighed. "I was never a spook. A spook is a spy like a CIA field operative. I was FBI. 'Was' is the key word – now being retired."

I nudged his arm. "Aw come on. Shell out," I said knowing that he liked '40s slang.

Larry was silent for a long time and then spoke in his serious low voice. "Josiah, I am very fond of you, but you always pitch a curve at me. Okay, here's the skinny. After what happened at the barn, I ameched a buddy of mine still working at the Bureau. I wanted a profile on O'nan. Some strings were pulled and O'nan's files were sent to him. It was astonishing." He turned to look at me. "None of this was your fault. If it hadn't been you, something else would have surely triggered O'nan to climb in your pocket. O'nan was a bad egg from the beginning. He should have never been allowed into any type of law enforcement. O'Nan is an obsessive compulsive with a narcissistic attitude accompanied by a nice strain of paranoia. Add a nasty temper to that and you've got a bad ass on your hands if you ruffle his feathers. He is smart, attentive to details and has turned to the dark. You've got a real problem on your hands if he is still alive. The only way for this to be resolved is if one of you is dead."

"Tell me something I don't know."

"What's the daughter doing about this?"

"She's got people looking for him 24/7, but that didn't stop someone from paying George Frank to make my life miserable. Shaneika has pulled out."

"I think that's smart. You're a walking bull's-eye."

"Thanks. Larry, would leaving town help?"

"He'd just shag you. Nope. You've got to be smart. If he's alive, make him come to you." Larry pointed a finger at me. "Now I've come as clean as a peeled egg. That's all I can say. Trap him and make it stick with the law."

It's no easy thing to be told you have to kill a man and that's what Larry was telling me. I didn't think O'nan had died and he was not going to tire of chasing me. I was his obsession now and the only way to get rid of him was to put him in the ground. I didn't know if I could live with the guilt of trapping and killing a man. Maybe I would just let him kill me. What was moral? What was right? What was doable? I would think about that tomorrow.

But then things changed later. They usually do.

I answered the phone late in the evening as I usually did.

"I've got some good news."

"Can't you say 'Hello Mother, how was your day?'"

As usual she ignored me. "I had a buddy of mine at Homeland Security put O'nan's picture in the facial recognition software and they got a positive hit. It seems like the heat was too much for O'nan since his friend squealed on him, and he boarded a plane for Brazil."

"So he's alive."

"Maybe. That software is not one hundred percent accurate."

"No extradition in Brazil still?"

"We have a treaty with Brazil, but they are very lax about it unless it suits their agenda. I'm sending a guy down to confirm it, but I'd say things can ease up a little bit. We're very close to confirming that O'nan's alive."

"Where's he getting his money?"

"I haven't discovered that yet, but I'm working on it."

"Coming home soon?"

"I'll be home before you know it."

Then that awful click.

"Gotta go. Love you." And then silence.

# 20

My daughter reported that no trace of O'nan could be found and the Bluegrass area was scoped again. Nothing. Since we had reason to believe that the immediate danger was over for a short while, Jake took a few needed days off. But I felt encouraged when he left. I could not become dependent on a bodyguard nor anyone else. I was going to become as self-reliant as possible.

Besides, I couldn't think when Jake was around. He seemed to fill the house with his voice, his smell and his physical presence. I found myself doing what he wanted just to please him. Now, really – does that sound like me?

Cody had come back and settled in, much to his chagrin. He was much easier to manage than Jake. Needing to take more control, I talked Cody into letting me drive to the mall. I gave him the doctor's written notification that I could drive within certain parameters. The fear of my having seizures was over.

Again, I had to check in every half hour. I had to be home within two hours. I had to stay where there were people around. Blah, blah, blah.

It's not that I had any intention of being bad. It's not that I had the intention of making either Jake or Cody angry. It's not that I had any intention of lying. It's that I had the intention of taking those steps toward liberty without anyone's permission. I felt it was my duty to be independent, to be self-reliant if I could. I knew the past year had been a strain on my daughter – both emotionally and financially. Matt had driven himself into depression with countless hours of work and worry. My problems had become a wedge between him and Franklin. I was becoming emotionally attached to Jake, which I'm sure was unwelcome. Don't all women become besotted with their protectors? I needed to speed up the recovery process so I could set everyone free. And I needed to find out what had happened to Jamie. Something drove that fifteen-year-old boy out on the river in the middle of the night. What was it?

I pulled carefully out of the driveway, but instead of heading for town, I turned the other way and headed for the ferry. Within fifteen minutes, I was safely across the river and speeding toward Richmond.

Once in Richmond, I looked at the sweaty piece of paper that Sarah had given me. I took out a map and checked for the street. Assured that I knew where I was going, I pulled out into the busy Richmond traffic on Main St. Seeing the street I needed, I turned sharply, much to the irritation of the gentleman behind, who gave me the single-finger dance. I traveled for another several miles before I came to my destination. I pulled the car up to the church so close that I touched its wall with my bumper. Oops! Still a little shaky at this driving.

Grasping my city stick, I walked up the handicapped ramp and entered the church by the side door. The church secretary, who had heard the old-fashioned bell on top of the door, met me. Apparently the bell was their only security measure. I must not have looked threatening as she readily told me where to find Ison Taggert . . . but not before I had a long talk with her.

Her name was Mrs. Bell and she was as old as Methuselah. She told me some very interesting stuff when I related that the family had some questions about Jamie Dunne's death. I love ancient nosy, talkative secretaries. They know everybody's business. And if they are silly, shallow women, like Mrs. Bell, who felt the need to be important – why they will tell a stranger anything and everything. What luck for me! The telephone rang and she left me hardly breathing I was so excited about the information I had gleaned.

My left leg was starting to give me fits so I hit it with my fist. That sometimes calmed the muscle twitches. Worked like a charm, so I hobbled down a few steps to the choir practice room. There I found Mr. Taggert putting new choir robes on hangers.

"Mr. Taggert," I said. "My name is Josiah Reynolds. I am a friend of Sarah Dunne's."

Ison Taggert was a tall man wearing the thick glasses of someone who had serious sight issues. He lifted his bifocals up on his nose to peer at me. There was a deep crease across its bridge. Turning his back on me, he fumbled with some hangers. "Really? Her son passed away several months ago and I don't remember you at the funeral," he said in a high unpleasant voice.

*How dare he turn his back to me! This was odd behavior to a woman with a cane. Most Kentucky men would have offered a chair.*

"I was incognito," I smarted off. "Irene Meckler, Jamie's aunt, has some questions about how he died and wanted me to help find some answers. If you don't mind, my visit will only take a few moments of your time." I looked around for a chair. "May I sit down, please?"

"I don't know how I can help you. I don't even know that I should be speaking to you. Never seen you before. Is this Ms. Meckler a member of our church?" Taggert asked, pulling a robe out of its plastic packaging.

"I thought that Mrs. Dunne had called and told you that I might be stopping by one day."

"Maybe. Maybe not."

I didn't understand this guy's hostility. Maybe he just didn't like women. Maybe he didn't like me. Maybe he was trying to stall because he was afraid of questions being asked. Maybe he was guilty of something.

He started to say something else, but I interrupted him. "Let's cut the crap, okay. I'm going to get right to the point. I understand that you gave Jamie a vintage Farrah Fawcett poster – the real thing, not a knock-off."

"What wrong with that?" Taggert said, hanging up another robe. He was avoiding eye contact.

"I never said anything was wrong with that. Just stating a fact. I would appreciate it if you would turn and face me."

He turned with a sullen expression on his pasty face. The last guy who was hostile tried to kill me. I wasn't taking my eyes off this s.o.b. for one second. If he took one step closer, I was going to crack his skull with my walking stick. I put my hand in my pocket and patted my taser before turning off the safety switch.

"Did he ever talk to you about his plans?"

"Like what?" He stood with his hand on his hip.

"How about plans to burn down a vineyard."

"Of course not."

"Then what did the two of you talk about? I have been told by several people that the two of you spent a good deal of time together."

"Our conversations are confidential," he smirked.

"Actually, they're not, Mr. Taggert. I gotta tell you that this looks odd. I'm a sick woman trying to tie some loose ends for the dead boy's mother and you are giving me attitude for no reason. Not to mention that you are in your forties and have never been married. No current girlfriend and you spend a lot of time with boys from your church. Classic."

"Now see here," he said, kicking a robe out of his way. "I'm into girls. Don't you start accusing me of something 'cause I'll sue."

"I see a middle-aged man who is a youth minister of a very conservative church wearing expensive jewelry, with dyed hair and capped teeth. You come across as less than sincere. In fact you drink too much and play the ponies."

"How dare you make such accusations?"

"I'm just repeating what I was told," I said, lifting my eyes to the ceiling.

He lifted his eyes as well and made the tattletale connection.

"Did you ever give Jamie some sex magazines?"

He paused.

"If you don't start telling me something, I'm going to go the church's superior and lay down some awful tales of innuendo. Now I want some answers. What did Jamie Dunne confide to you?"

Taggert hissed, "He was concerned about his mother. She had financial worries that he felt the Golden Sun Vineyard were responsible for."

"You are lying. The Silver Creek Vineyard had no such financial worries."

"I swear to you. I am telling you what he told me. He said his mother was in substantial debt."

"What else?"

"That's all."

"Did you give him condoms? Try to bond with him over some dirty magazines?"

Taggert hesitated. His shiny forehead glistened with drops of sweat. "He wanted to know about sex. He was curious, so I counseled him."

"By giving him dirty magazines with twisted images? That's not your job. You're a youth minister. That is all that you are."

"You're wrong. This church does not address the concerns of its youth. It is way behind the times. I am the only person that these boys have to talk with. They have no one else."

"Did you give Jamie Dunne condoms?"

"No, of course not."

"His partner said he got them from someone in this church. I think that person was you. Whether you did or not, I'm going to speak with the pastor."

"Look, if you do that, these young people will just learn off the street. If Jamie was given condoms, it was by someone who was looking out for him. Trying to protect him."

"Jamie was fifteen years old. He had no business being inducted into adult sex by a church figure whose job it was to insulate him from such conduct. Look, I'm not an old fuddy-duddy. I understand how the world works, what drives us as human beings. I know we are programmed to reproduce, but you have no idea the problems that have been caused by you giving Jamie the green light to have sex. He got a young girl pregnant and now her life is going to be painful no matter what she decides to do about this baby."

"You can't prove anything. I'll sue you."

"I've got those magazines and a condom wrapper. And now I am going to tear his room apart to find more. If I find one of your sweaty fingerprints on those magazine pages, then I am going to turn it over to the police. You'll have a hell of a time – it's called corrupting a minor. Then I'm going to ask them to reopen his file. Perhaps, Jamie was going to tell on you and you killed him to keep him quiet. You would have lost your position – everything. You would have been disgraced."

Taggert stumbled toward me and gasped. "You can't be serious. His death was an accident. I . . . I'll take a lie detector test; anything, but I had nothing to do with that boy's death. I loved him. I would never have harmed him. I may be many things, but I did not hurt that boy or cause his death." He began choking, "Don't you . . . dare suggest that. Don't you dare!"

He grabbed his left arm and fell back upon a chair with a thud. A thick sweat broke out upon his brow. "I think I'm having a heart attack," he rasped.

Alarmed, I hobbled over to the stairwell to call the secretary, but Mrs. Bell had already called 911 as she had been listening as I suggested. I hurriedly unbuttoned Taggert's shirt and pants. The secretary shuffled as fast as she could with a blanket. We both waited, holding Taggert's hands until the ambulance came.

"I'd better go with him," Mrs. Bell said, practically smacking her dry lips. I could see her already rehearsing the story and deciding whom to tell first.

"What you need to do is call your pastor and the both of you search Taggert's office or any place that would be good for hiding things. If you don't and this guy has really has had a heart attack, then you, the church and I can be sued by this creep."

Her hand flew to her mouth. "Oh goodness. We don't want that. What shall we be looking for?"

"You'll know it when you find it, but I would check his computer, desk and his car. I would even pull the paneling from the wall. Look up in the ceiling. And make sure you don't get your fingerprints on what you find. Or he could say it was yours to begin with. I'll go to the hospital and let you know how he's doing."

"Oh dear, this is all so alarming." Mrs. Bell gave me a look that told me she regretted confiding in me. She knew Taggert was a creep, but at least it had been calm before I walked into their quaint little church.

Too bad. That's how I looked at it.

I checked in at the emergency room telling them that I was Taggert's aunt and was allowed into his cubicle. I peeped between curtains and, seeing he was not there, took the opportunity to search his pants, which were hanging on a chair. I just found change, twenty-three dollars and his car keys. Hoping that Mrs. Bell had had more success, I called the church.

Mrs. Bell answered.

"Find anything yet?" I asked, crossing my fingers.

"I'll let you talk to the pastor," she replied, muffling the phone.

"Uh oh," I thought. I hoped I wasn't going to be scolded.

"Hello, who's this?" asked an authoritative deep bass voice.

"Mrs. Reynolds. Who is this?"

"This is Brother Morris. How are you connected to our youth minister?"

I gave him a brief rundown on how I had been asked to look into Jamie Dunne's death and my theory on who had given the boy the dirty magazines and condoms.

"So you see it was just a process of elimination. His reaction was hostile from the get-go. No one else was like that. It has to be him. Did you find anything?"

There was a slight pause.

"Brother Morris. Please don't cover anything up. If you have found something, then you have a wolf among your sheep. It will cause you nothing but grief if you try to put a lid on this, because I'll be behind stirring the pot."

He took a deep breath. "You will keep this confidential until the church can formulate a plan of action?"

"Yes sir."

"We found church property in the trunk of his car and several boxes of condoms in his locker."

"He can say those condoms are for his use."

"Either way, it's bad. Our church doesn't approve of pre-marital sex. We don't hire staff that won't abide by our policies. We called in one of our members to go over the church computers and a locksmith to unlock his car."

"That is an illegal search on his car."

"The church financed the car for him and the loan has not been paid off yet – so technically, the church owns the car. Also one of our members is an officer on the Richmond police force. He is on his way over – in an unofficial capacity, of course. Some other members are searching Taggert's office and the choir room. Once they report back to me, I will call the deacons of the church and together we will decide what to do."

There was static on the phone. He was pacing as he talked. "This is most unsettling. Most unsettling."

By this time, I had walked back into the emergency waiting room while talking on the cell phone. A nurse motioned for me to turn the phone off. "Just make sure that whatever is found, you are very careful handling it. You don't want your fingerprints on anything or else it can turn on you."

"I will make sure everyone understands this."

I heard someone call the minister's name.

"Look, I gotta go. If you see Brother Taggert, tell him that I will be there in a couple of hours. After all, he is still a member of our flock and I am his shepherd."

"Sure thing," I replied, but I had no intention of seeing Taggert. After I hung up, I approached the nurses' desk.

"I am Mr. Taggert's relative. Is there any news on him yet?"

The nurse looked at her computer screen. "I think an evaluation is just about finished. He is being relocated to a semi-private room now. Let me call his doctor for you." She made the call. Within a few minutes, she ushered me into a private consultation room.

A young emergency room doctor strode into the room and shook my hand. He looked nine. "Because of our guidelines, I can't go into specifics, but your nephew is resting comfortably and should be released tomorrow morning. We are keeping him for observation, just in case."

I blinked. "You're letting him go tomorrow? You let people who have had heart attacks leave the hospital less that twenty-four hours after admittance?"

The doctor sighed. "I really shouldn't be discussing this with you."

"He doesn't have a wife, just kinfolk. We need to know how to help. Please don't keep us in the dark," I pleaded, my eyes threatening to cry. I rummaged through my purse looking for a handkerchief.

"I can assure you that Mr. Taggert has not had a heart attack."

"Really? It looked like a heart attack."

"It was simply a bad stress attack which can sometimes mimic a heart attack. But these stress attacks can be serious. He will need to take it easy for the next couple of days."

"I can assure you, Doctor, that I will do everything possible to stay out of his way for the next couple of days. I think his minister will be here within the next hour."

The doctor smiled. "That will be good. Having a comforting presence is always good for the patient."

I stood and shook hands with the doctor. I could have kissed him. I could have danced a little jig if my leg had not been hurting so. A little stress attack was not a major lawsuit, especially if the church kept finding icky stuff. I was almost in the clear legally.

Walking out of the emergency room, I realized I was a major cynic. The truth was I didn't care what happened to Taggert as long as it didn't involve me. He was just taking up space as far as I was concerned. He was one of those careless people that F. Scott Fitzgerald wrote about. It wasn't that I didn't think adults shouldn't provide some sort of guidance for teenagers; it was that I found his methods too raw and primitive for sensitive young boys. He either didn't understand the consequences of his actions or didn't care. Either way, he was dangerous to young minds.

Or was it just Jamie that got special treatment? Was Taggert jealous? As a plain man, he could have been envious of Jamie's good looks and youth. Did he want to destroy the boy's happiness by putting ridiculous thoughts into his head such as burning down a winery and having sex with the hired help? Each episode would have blighted Jamie's Huckleberry Finn existence and tarnished his relationship with his loving mother.

The truth about Jamie would never be known. He left no written record nor trusted any friend with his thoughts. Did he have sex with Bloomie because of Taggert's unnatural influence? Or did he actually care for her? Even Bloomie didn't really know. Now he was dead and she was in a bad way.

And I was in a bad way.

I was an hour late returning home, and I hadn't checked in, plus I had turned my cell phone off.

Cody must be frantic, especially if he tried to locate me through the GPS on my hearing aid and discovered that I was in a hospital. I needed to get home.

Checking my phone, I found four messages. I called Cody's cell phone from the parking lot.

Jake answered. "Why the hell are you in a hospital?"

Startled, I almost dropped the phone. "I'm coming home right now. I can explain."

"You stay right there. I'm coming for you."

"No, I'm coming home." I hung up. Boy oh boy, was I going to be in big trouble. I felt nauseous and my body was racked with pain. I needed my medication.

I kept a secret pill in my wallet in case of emergencies. Pulling it out, I rolled it in my palm, sitting in the car looking out at the parking lot. Silently and with great regret, I put it back in my wallet.

Something was calling me to the river. I was already in trouble. I might as well go for the brass ring. I felt a pressing need to get on the water. I massaged my right leg. It was limber enough to allow me to drive, so I took the old Tates Creek Road home slowly and arrived at the Butterfly without incident. Once home, I went inside to get my files on Jamie and then drove down to the dock.

Thank goodness neither Jake nor Cody were home. They were probably on I-75 hoping to intercept me. It wouldn't take them long to realize their mistake and head home. I had to get on that pontoon boat before they could catch me. Something was tumbling around in my mind about what someone had said. I knew if I could catch it and study it in my mind's eye, I could solve the mystery. But what was it?

I was now in full-blown agony. Reaching up under my shirt, I pulled off the pain patch and threw it on the floor. It had been used up. Each bump in the road caused me to groan as a wave of pain slapped over me. Finally, I made it to the dock. Throwing open the car door, I grabbed my purse, my cane and the files, and snatched the boat key from its hidden place. Limping severely now, almost dragging my left foot, I undid the pontoon lines and crawled on board.

Something was really wrong. Even with the pain patch used up, I should have had some residual pain medication in my body. Was Jake giving me fake pain patches so he could wean me off the pain medication? What a time to discover that! Still, I wouldn't give up. I took my pain pill out and broke it in half, knowing my mind would still be sharp enough with half a pill. I forced it down, swallowing it dry.

Starting the boat, I eased it from the dock and down the quiet river. Sitting in the captain's chair with my legs extended gave me some relief as I putt-putted down the green ribbon of river, which had once been a mighty commercial thoroughfare and now largely forgotten. I made it without incident to the Silver Creek dock. Turning the boat off, I sat down and studied my notes.

Hearing a noise, I looked up to see a young man who worked for Sarah, investigating my presence. As the pontoon boat was starting to drift, I threw him the lines. "Can you ask Miss Sarah to come to me, please?" I asked. "I need to speak with her."

He scratched his ginger hair. "Well, she's real busy right now."

"I SAID GO GIT HER, BOY! NOW!"

Startled, he replied, "Okay, but you don't need to be so rude."

My teeth were grinding. "Go on. Fetch her for me."

Several minutes later, Sarah hurried down the hill. Climbing into the boat, she seemed anxious and bewildered. "Is anything wrong?"

"Other than feeling like road kill, no. Have a seat for a minute. I need to ask you a question that has been on my mind for some time."

Sarah obediently sat, looking at me wild-eyed.

"You tell me that you are financially solvent. Business has been slow, but you are not in any major debt that would have caused Jamie to worry."

She nodded.

"Then why do I hear rumors that you are in debt?"

"Who told you that?"

"It doesn't matter. Are you in trouble financially?"

Sarah leaned forward. "The only thing I have is a standard $30,000 business loan which I take out every year because of a cash flow problem in the early spring, but the loan is always paid back by December. It's just a standard business loan because I don't want to dip into my savings."

"Did Jamie understand that?"

"He didn't know anything about it. Why would he?"

"Could he have stumbled upon some loan papers or heard you on the phone with a loan officer? You know $30,000 sounds like an awful lot to a kid. He could have misunderstood."

Sarah's hand flew to her mouth. "Oh dear. Thinking back now, there was something. They got my payment book wrong again for the third time in a row this year, so I called the bank manager and gave him what for. Maybe Jamie overhead me."

"Were you angry, maybe talking loud to the bank manager?"

"Yes, I just gave him heck on the phone. I was frustrated that I had to keep correcting the payment book."

"Sarah, I think Jamie overheard you on the phone." I stopped myself from saying anything else. It didn't take an Einstein to realize the likely sequence of events.

Sarah sat back in her chair staring at me for several minutes until realization illuminated her sorrowful eyes. "Oh no. You must be wrong. He wouldn't jump to that conclusion, would he? It was just a stupid loan. It was nothing. Oh my poor baby." She looked at me with alarm. "It was just a simple loan. I was just angry about the paperwork not being correct. Jamie. Jamie. Why?" Sarah threw her head into her worn hands.

Out of the corner of my eye, I saw Bloomie running down the hill. "He thought by burning down the vines of your competitor, he was helping you. It was just being teenage dumb. He did it out of love, Sarah. He did it out of love."

Bloomie climbed onto the boat.

"Help her into the house, Bloomie, and stay with her. She'll tell you what's wrong in her own good time. Perhaps, you might have something to share with her as well. Just a thought," I said.

Bloomie helped Sarah up the hill and turning, she looked at me with doubtful eyes.

A blue heron flew over. Somewhere a horse neighed. The river rhythmically lapped upon the shores. The music created by the waves sounded almost happy. But then, the river was happy. Jamie loved the river. The river had returned Jamie's love, and like a selfish lover, she had laid claim to him. I knew the river held the secrets to my questions. Could I get the river goddess to give them up?

I started the boat and headed down the water. Traveling several miles, I turned off the boat and let it drift slowly. Something was still nagging at me. I reread the files, paying close attention to the newspaper accounts. Closing my eyes, I replayed every conversation I had had concerning Jamie. A half hour later, my eyelids fluttered open. I knew. Yes, I knew what had happened to Jamie Dunne.

# 21

Still, I had to be sure. There might be some physical evidence I could discover. But I could not go beyond that. I would have to tell Irene my theory and let her take it from there . . . if she wanted to. And there was a chance I could be wrong. I was about to turn the boat around when I spied Rodney Tavis' boat tied up to a tree. It was empty. I cast around looking for Tavis, but he seemed nowhere near. Pulling on the limbs of trees near the bank, I swung the pontoon boat near his.

This was stupid, I told myself. I had no backup. But it might be my only chance to know for sure, the devil on my left shoulder whispered to me. Getting closer, I inspected the fishing boat. Reaching out, I pulled on the boat's rope bringing it next to the pontoon boat. Carefully I climbed into the rocking fishing boat. I searched but found nothing. Then I ran my hand on the outside of the boat feeling for scratches or dents. Success! I found a large dent on the right side. Leaning over, I saw some kind of paint. Thrusting my hand about in a rusty toolbox, I found a knife, which I used to scrape the dented area, and placed the residue in a handkerchief from my pocket.

"Whadda ya think you're doing?"

My head jerked up.

Rod Tavis was standing on the bank with his shotgun folded in his arms. He looked big and mean.

I heard the devil laughing. "I was loo . . . looking for you," I stuttered, stuffing the handkerchief in my pocket.

"Why?"

"I wanted to ask more questions about Jamie Dunne."

"Like I said. Never saw him that night."

I swallowed. "Okay. I best be going then." I started to climb back into my boat.

Rod Tavis made a quick move with his foot and pushed the pontoon boat out of my reach. "Whatcha got in your pocket?"

"Nothing."

"I saw you scrape my boat. Whadja do that for?"

I couldn't think of anything to reply so I kept quiet.

"Cat got your tongue, lady?"

"Please, my leg is hurting awful bad. Let me go to my boat."

He shook his head "You act like you got something on me. So until you tell, you gonna stay with me." He pulled his boat line toward him.

I almost fell from the rocking boat into the river – with all those river snakes. Yuk!

"You met Jamie Dunne on the river!" I blurted. "It was an accident, but you killed him nevertheless. You said you never saw him that night. The paper makes no reference to what part of the day Jamie drowned but that his body was found in the morning. Only the person who would know that he was out at night was the person who killed him."

Tavis' eyes narrowed as he swung around his shotgun. "You don't know nothing."

"I know and Sarah Dunne knows too. I told her about an hour ago, so you holding me here won't help you. She'll call the police if I don't return in half an hour."

"Lots can happen in thirty minutes."

"Like what?"

"You can have an accident."

"Like Jamie? I think you didn't mean to harm him. You were watching your fishnets, trying to catch the person who was stealing from you. You see Jamie. Maybe his kayak got tangled up in them. Anyway, you confront him. He denies it, but he's in a hurry to get away. This just increases your belief that he is guilty. He is really trying to get away from a fire he had started, but you didn't know that. You try to stop him and his kayak turns over accidentally. Jamie comes back up furious, and in the melee, hits his head on your boat and drowns because he wasn't wearing his life jacket.

"Those dents, on your boat, have paint on them. I think the test results will show that it is paint from Jamie's kayak."

"That's not going to happen as no test is going to be taken. You step up here now."

"I can't. I won't."

He turned the gun around with the butt ready to knock me up side the head. Before the wood made contact, I jumped into the chilly water and began swimming toward the Jessamine County side of the river. My strokes were swift and sure. Thank God, Jake had me swim for months. I didn't even think about the cold water rippling across my face. Then I heard the boat's motor start up. Fast as I was, I would never make it to the shore in time, as the current was too fast and pulling me downstream. Looking over my shoulder, I could see Tavis was gaining on me.

Suddenly Brannon was before me, floating on top of the water. "Now?"

I thought, *Get the hell out of my way, Brannon. For the last time, I'm not coming.*

Brannon gave me a disappointed look before he sank below the river current.

Feeling something brush against my leg, I turned my head to see a water snake wiggle away from me. I gasped and started to go down.

"REACH OUT!"

Instinctively my hand shot out and felt a rough rope bobbing on the water. Grabbing it, I was immediately pulled toward shore. My eyes closed as I sped through the water until my feet began making contact with the rocks and debris in the riverbed. Then two strong hands pulled at my hair and shirt, dragging me up on the riverbank. Coughing, I attempted to wipe the water from my burning eyes until I puked and began choking on my own vomit. Someone turned me over and wiped out my mouth with their fingers looking for river debris. Then someone hit me on the back, causing me to spit out a lump of half-decayed leaves. Exhausted, I laid my head down on a bed of vomit, wet leaves and river stones.

Another boat was coming down the river – fast.

I flopped over on my side and saw Tavis look toward the other boat and then veer his boat to the west, disappearing around a bend. The motor became louder until it cut off abruptly. Jake was on the prow of my rusty johnboat holding an assault rifle while Cody manned its ancient motor. As the boat made contact with the bank, Jake threw the gun to Cody and jumped onto the shore. In three long strides he was beside me and pulled me into a sitting position, pushing my wet hair back. "Are you all right?"

"I think so. Just scared." My chest was heaving.

"Here, take this," he said, trying to push the abuterol spray into my mouth.

I pushed it away. "I'm okay. Really. Just give me a minute." Slowly my heavy breathing began to subside.

"Can you talk?"

I nodded, letting him take my pulse. "I jumped in the water, but couldn't make it to the shore fast enough.

Someone threw me a lifeline – literally a rope pulling me to shore. Saved me from Tavis."

"Who was it?"

"I couldn't see, but I think it was Moshe Goren."

Cody was now hanging over me. He held the rope. "Look at it. It's homemade from natural fibers."

"It seems like your Boo Radley has appointed himself as your guardian angel," smiled Jake.

I returned his smile. "I have many angels on my side," I replied, pressing his hand.

For once Cody did not look bored. "Let's get you home," he said.

Since I still wasn't my college weight, I pooh-poohed the idea of one of them carrying me to the pontoon boat. I made it on my own steam with occasional help.

Cody tied the johnboat to the back of the pontoon boat.

Jake stood at the bow scanning the banks, holding his rifle. His black hair fluttered in the wind.

For the first time I noticed he had let it grow out from its military crew cut. It looked unruly . . . and sexy. It gave me pleasure to imagine Jake dressed in feathers and war paint, or tight jeans with a soft, white cotton shirt rolled up to the elbows and opened at the throat . . . or nothing at all.

For the first time in many years, I really cared about how I looked. I glanced down. Covered in mud, I smelled like a wet dog. I had lost my shoes and my wet summer dress clung to me exposing the last of my fat rolls. *Oh dear,* I thought. *That damn river wants me like it wanted Jamie.* I almost died again, but I'm thinking that it's time to dust off my high heels and give life one last spin before the river claims me.

I looked down at the dark, green river being sliced in two by the boat making its way back home. I looked again at Jake's stern profile and felt safe.

He turned to check on me. His expression softened when I gave him a thumbs-up.

The river wouldn't get me today. I smiled at the fading sun.

Life surely takes strange turns.

\*

I was safely tucked in bed watching *Jaws* when the phone rang.

"Where are you?"

"In the States. I'm coming home."

"Good. We need to talk."

"I hear you had a successful day. Don't tell me the details but you're happy?"

"Not happy, but satisfied. Irene came over and I gave my story to her. I filed an assault report against Rod Tavis for myself, but what she does with her information is up to her."

"I also hear that you caused a man to have a stress attack so severe he thought he had a heart attack?"

"Yeah. I'm rather pleased with myself. Like I said, it's been a successful day."

"Hmmmm. Like going AWOL."

"If we talk about that, then we will have to delve into Afghanistan."

"I was in Amsterdam."

"Sure you were."

"Changing the subject. My team traced someone who looked like O'nan to a small town in Brazil but he disappeared after the twentieth of this month. No sightings anywhere."

"Could he be in Lexington?"

"Doubt it, but you might want to think twice about ditching your bodyguard team again."

There was a click on the line. "Gotta go. See you in a couple of days."

Dead air.

# 22

I was working at the Farmers' Market when Shaneika surprised me. "Howdy," I said, happy to see her. I wanted her to come back to the farm. I missed seeing Comanche in the fields, and having Shaneika stop by for coffee and verbally wrangle with Jake over history.

"I've got the city's response to the lawsuit," she said solemnly. "These are the terms." She hand me a folder.

My hands were shaking as I opened it. I skimmed over the highlighted parts and looked at her in disbelief. "Is this accurate? They agree to the stuff highlighted in yellow?"

"Yes, they did. You were right. The mayor wants to run for governor and doesn't want you mucking that up with interviews two years from now or writing a book about O'nan," she said.

"You know that for sure?"

"Let's say I surmised that from listening to two secretaries gossiping in the ladies' room who didn't realize I was in a stall."

"Thank you Jesus. Thank you."

"No – thank me. Jesus wasn't at the negotiating table. Here's your first check." She handed me a check for a million and a half dollars. This was the first installment. "Once you endorse this check, you can never publicly make any type of statement disparaging the police department or the city regarding this incident. You can never discuss the details of the settlement with the city or what happened the night you were attacked."

"Give me a pen. I'll sign the check right now. I don't care who is to blame. I just need to pay my medical bills, and not worry about the future if my health goes south."

I began to cry. I was solvent again. "I gotta go to the bank," I said, tearing off my apron. I frantically looked around for my purse.

"Slow down or you'll fall," advised Shaneika. "My son will watch your booth while I drive you to the bank."

"Your son?"

Behind Shaneika emerged a young boy. He smiled with perfect white teeth like his mother.

I offered my hand. "I'm Mrs. Reynolds and you are?"

"Lincoln Warfield Clark Todd. Everyone calls me Linc." He took my hand and shook it. His hands were warm and dry – full of living energy. They felt good to touch. "This is gonna be great. I've been watching you and I know what to do. When you get back, I'll have everything packed up for you. Yeah. This is gonna be great."

"Okay, you're in charge. If you will hand me my purse, I'll be off. Oh, will you tell Mr. Dosh, when he comes back, where I've gone? He looks like Sitting Bull with a grudge on a bad hair day."

"A real Indian! Cool," replied Linc, grinning.

"My car is over there," said Shaneika. "Let's get that check in the bank. The bank's only open twenty more minutes. It makes me nervous to have that much money based on a small piece of paper that can get lost or stolen."

We hopped into her SUV and sped down the few blocks to the bank.

On the way over, Shaneika didn't offer any details on her son, so I didn't ask.

I deposited the check five minutes before the bank closed.

Shaneika told me to hang on to the receipt.

I put it down my bosom causing Shaneika to grimace and mouth the word "nasty." I thought it was the safest place in town.

# 23

A knock sounded on Officer Kelly's front door.

A dark-haired woman, with two small children trailing behind her, went to answer. She peered through the peephole, backed up in surprise and then opened the door tentatively. "Can I help you?" she asked.

A tall woman, with black hair pulled into a sleek ponytail trailing down her back, stood at the door. She was dressed in a black leather car coat with black pants and black ankle boots. To complete the outfit, she was wearing dark aviator sunglasses and large diamond post earrings.

On the street waited a black Expedition with a driver.

"Are you Batman's wife?" asked the older of the two boys.

The stranger gave a thin-lipped smile. "Cute." She turned her attention to the mother. "I am . . ."

"I . . . know who you are," replied Mrs. Kelly. "He's not here. He's at Al's Bar working on his poems."

The stranger appraised the woman who had taken her place in Kelly's affections, noticing that they both looked very similar.

Both were dark. Both were beautiful. Both were extremely athletic. Both were dangerous when crossed. But only one had found happiness.

"I know where he is. I wanted to meet you. And give you this." A gloved hand extended an envelope. "Go on. Take it. It's from my mother. Payment for Baby's bills."

Mrs. Kelly gingerly took the thick envelope all the while wondering if she should accept it. The woman standing before her disturbed her. The stranger was overly confident and Mrs. Kelly could see that she was used to getting her way. One could say life's rules did not apply. The very air moved through her instead of around like for normal people. She did not take up space; she moved through it. Mrs. Kelly rocked on her heels. So this was the famous . . . or infamous, depending on who was doing the talking – Asa Reynolds.

The stranger started to turn, but stopped. "Oh, my mother also expects to be invited for dinner soon. Ciao." Giving the children once last look, the stranger walked back to the car, her boots clicking loudly on the sidewalk pavement.

Mrs. Kelly closed the door in mute surprise. The envelope was addressed to her. She sat on the couch and opened it with her two children clamoring beside her in anticipation.

Inside was a warm, personal note from Josiah, a letter from Josiah's lawyer, Shaneika Mary Todd, explaining the contents and an itemized statement of the vet's bill plus estimated costs of Baby's stay with the Kellys. A gift tin dropped from the envelope. Opening it, she discovered a personal gift card loaded with the amount of $20,000. She crossed herself.

"What is it, Mommy?" asked one little boy, surprised at his mother's flushed face.

"The answer to my prayers," she replied. "My babies gonna get new shoes! And Mommy is going to replace the furniture that the monster dog chewed up and buy something pretty for herself for puttin' up with Daddy." The boys looked curiously at the little plastic card, but squealed with delight as their mother tickled their bellies.

\*

On the other side of town, the black sedan waited on Limestone.

Ready to go home, Kelly walked out of Al's Bar with a notebook full of poems. Whistling the tune *Hi Ho* sung by the seven dwarfs from Snow White, he made a beeline for his vehicle.

Several homeless guys, whom he occasionally arrested for disorderly conduct, good-naturedly called out in greeting.

Kelly waved to them.

Inside the sedan, Josiah's daughter watched Officer Kelly cross the street and unlock his car. She sat silently in the back seat as he drove off. Fingering a recent newspaper account that told how Officer Kelly caught a bank robber by noticing disturbed moss on a pathway, she watched his car disappear around the corner. Carefully, she folded the newspaper article and put it in her wallet, next to Kelly's high school senior picture.

Finally her driver asked, "Where to, ma'am?"

"Home," she rasped sadly. "Take me home."

# 24

Standing outside the massive twin doors, I collected my thoughts. Did I really want to do this?

I raised my hand to knock on the carved wood and then dropped it, looking back to the black limo waiting for me. Even though I couldn't forgive, the acts of forgiveness could begin and maybe somewhere down the line I could emotionally follow their trail. I knocked on the door, barely making a sound, as I hoped no one would come to answer.

An older woman opened the door, glancing at me with my shopping bags sitting by my feet while I leaned on my black walking stick. "My name is Josiah Reynolds," I said to her. "I don't have an appointment but I would like to see Miss Ellen."

The woman looked confused, not knowing what to do. I knew that she recognized my name.

"Is there somewhere I can sit down," I asked. "My leg is really hurting!" That line always seemed to do the trick and this time it was true. She immediately let me inside and led me to a small parlor where uncomfortable, mid-nineteenth-century furniture was placed about. Probably family heirlooms. Too ugly to put in a frequented room, but too valuable to throw away. I sat in a walnut Washington Holloway chair.

Having fetched my shopping bags, the woman sat them by my feet and said she'd go to see if Miss Ellen was in – a nice way of saying Miss Ellen might not want to see me. She closed the painted pocket doors with ornamental gold painted on the white. I looked about the room trying to stifle the urge to swipe something – like a candy dish or silver candlestick.

My eyes turned to the marble fireplace where above the mantel hung a Frank Duveneck. My fingers rushed to my lips. It was the same Duveneck portrait that I had given Brannon on our last anniversary before we separated. It had cost me a whole year's pay. Now I knew what had happened to it.

He had turned around and given it to his girlfriend.

I felt a sudden giggle rush up my throat followed by an awful taste of bile. I thought I was going to be sick, hoping to vomit on the antique carpet, but then one of the doors slid open.

In stepped Ellen. She gave the room a quick glance before resting upon me.

I didn't rise. I was not in the mood to go out of my way anymore. There she stood, slightly quivering before making her way toward me.

Still fresh and beautiful in her last remaining years of youth, her brunette hair perfectly coiffed, she sat opposite me – silently disapproving.

"Why are you here, Josiah?" asked Ellen. She was tense.

I nudged one of the shopping bags toward her. "Inside these bags are things that belonged to Brannon. I thought the boy might want to have them. I put together an album of pictures from Brannon's youth until his death. Also there is his letter jacket from high school, his college ring, some letters – just bits and pieces of his life that the boy might want to keep as mementos."

Ellen tilted her head like a dog trying to comprehend.

"Inside the pocket of the letter jacket is a letter from your son's sister with a telephone number. If he wishes to see her, he may leave a message at that number. The number will be disconnected on his twenty-first birthday and the offer will be rescinded – forever."

I stood. "You may read the letter if you wish. I know that you and I will never see eye to eye on this, but the children don't need to suffer. He's the only sibling my daughter will ever have."

Ellen stood as well. "I don't know what to say. This is very decent of you, Josiah."

"I have my moments." Not knowing what else to convey, I started to leave. Suddenly I turned. "That's a nice Duveneck you have."

Her face became clouded as though she was both pleased and puzzled at my remark. "Yes, Brannon gave it to me when I learned that I was pregnant."

I gave it one last glance. "It is really a nice painting. Brannon always did have such elegant taste."

Ellen smiled wistfully while glancing at the painting. "Yes, he did," she said softly.

I turned and left the house.

Asa got out of the limo and helped me step up into the vehicle.

"How did it go?" she asked.

"I think she might let you see the boy," I answered. "Just give her some time to think about it. You should send him a gift this Christmas to start the ball rolling."

My daughter nodded and gave the driver instructions to drop us off at the Bluegrass Airport.

We boarded a chartered plane, which flew us to New Orleans, where we were met by Brannon's two surviving siblings. The four of us ventured out into the delta on a rented boat where we poured Brannon's ashes while playing his favorite piece, Robert Johnson's *Cross Road Blues*.

Afterwards, my in-laws promised to visit Kentucky with their families and bade a quick farewell while leaving Asa and myself to dip our beignets in café au lait at Café du Monde on Decatur St. There we silently watched the tourists and lovers stroll by.

I couldn't wait to get out. New Orleans was always a
city of death to me with its above-ground graveyards,
neglected mausoleums and mansions bathed in parasitic
vegetation. I could tell Asa was tense too.

Too many unhappy memories of us visiting Brannon's
relatives, and Brannon disappearing almost the entire
time to visit "friends."

New Orleans was always a city of disappointed trips
and unchallenged lies. Brannon, like his hometown,
promised much but in the end conveniently forgot.
Brannon was one of those careless people of Fitzgerald's.

Finally it was time for me to catch a plane back to
Lexington and Asa to fly to Washington for her next
assignment.

I did not feel forgiving. In fact, anger had been
simmering ever since I glimpsed that painting. I would
have to talk to Matt about this. He would give me a new
perspective on it. Maybe I would talk about it with Jake,
but I already knew what he would say. Let it go. Let it
go. Not worth the anger. Anger is bad for healing.

But I would hang on to my anger, letting it whiten to a
soft scar, hardening over time into a sinewy sliver.

Lexington was having one of its ferocious late spring
thunderstorms, the kind that carries tornadoes with them,
when Jake met me at the baggage area.

He was sporting a big smile.

I was surprised that my heart sped up when I saw him.

He said he wanted to have a private talk with me, so we
went to out to dinner even though I was very tired.

I could see that he had something on his mind.

I told him how the meeting with Ellen went.

He seemed pleased that it went well. Fidgeting with his silverware, he opened his mouth several times only to close it.

"Look, Jake. I'm going to fall asleep in about fifteen minutes regardless of where I am, so if there is something on your mind, you better tell me now." I took a sip of my water.

"I signed my new contract. It has been renewed for the next nine months after October."

"So you're going to stay," I said, suddenly frightened that I came close to losing him.

"If you want me to, I will. But there have to be some changes," Jake stated.

"Like what?"

"Now that your dead husband no longer lives in your closet, I thought you might be willing to move forward."

I sat looking at him, waiting.

Jake coughed, glancing about the room. "There is a powwow for Choctaws in Mississippi next week. I would like to go and take you with me."

I pulled out my planner from my purse. "I take it that this is going to be on a weekend. I think I can get Charles' daughter, Bess, to look after my booth at the Farmers' Market." I marked the calendar with a pencil. "If I can get her, then I can go. She'll take care of everything for me."

Jake grabbed the pencil out of my hand. "I don't think you understand."

I shrugged. "What do I not understand?"

He struggled to find the words. "Not like with Matt but with a man."

"Matt *is* a man."

"What I mean is not like a friend."

Realization dawned upon me. It was what I had hoped for but now the fantasy had to end.

"This is ridiculous. I'm too old for you."

"Aged like fine wine," he smiled.

I shook my head no. "It's impossible. I haven't thought that way about a man for years."

"You think that way about Matt. I've seen you look at him."

"Not that it is any of your damn business, but I love Matt. I love his beauty. I love his good manners. I love his loyalty. He was my only friend when everyone else turned their backs on me."

"I'm loyal."

"You're paid to be loyal."

"So don't pay me."

"How can I not pay you?" I lowered my voice as people were turning to stare. "I'm not healthy. My goodness, I can barely walk. I might have a deranged cop after my head. My childbearing years are past. There are just too many negatives with me. You need to be with a young woman. Someone who is whole and has energy. Someone who will make you a good wife, a good partner."

Jake moved his plate out of his way. "Look, I've thought about this. I've seen everything you've got, so there are no surprises with the body."

I could feel the blood rushing to my face.

"Here's what I see. Yes, you're a little worn around the edges but there is something about you that I just like. Don't ask me why. You're bossy and sarcastic. Maybe I just like a woman who's full of sass. And yes, you're struggling, but who isn't. Your face is not bad to look at either since the docs lined your cheekbones back up."

I leaned toward him and whispered into his ear. "I don't know if everything works. You understand?"

"You let me worry about that," Jake said with a lopsided grin on his face. His arm reached over and he began to stroke my arm. His touch made my arm hair stand to attention.

I tapped the table. "This is serious. That part of my life may be over for good. The thought of any kind of weight on my legs make me apoplectic. I don't think I can respond."

"Well, if you don't find me attractive, then we can end this conversation right now," muttered Jake, pulling away.

"I never said that. You know that's not it," I whispered, looking to see if people were still staring.

"What? Can't hear you. Speak up."

"I said that is not the case. I think you are very handsome . . . for being you."

"Okay, let's just go to Mississippi for the powwow. We will take it slow. We'll eat lots of fried bread, listen to the storytelling and buy crappy souvenirs. No expectations. We'll just have a good time. Separate rooms."

"Would this sudden interest in me have anything to do with the fact that I am now financially solvent?"

"It sure doesn't hurt."

"Who's paying for this trip?"

"I am, but the next one is on you. I have a hankering for Venice."

"What if we get serious and then you want children? What are we going to do then?"

"Already crossed that bridge. Have children."

"You do? Oh, are you married?"

"Nope. Divorced. The kids are going to be at the powwow." Jake rose while throwing three twenties on the table. "Well, you look plumb tuckered out," he said, looking at my stunned face. "Let's get you to bed. You've had a long day."

Picking up my purse and walking stick, he offered me his arm.

After hesitating for a moment, I took it and leaned on him as he led me out into the lightning storm that lit up a greenish sky that told of a coming tornado.

# EPILOGUE

I never saw Moshe Goren to thank him for saving me nor did he respond to my notes left at the beehives.

My daughter checked his cave and found it had been abandoned.

At this point, we are assuming he went back to New York. That is being verified.

My walking is better. I stumble less.

Jake decided I needed to take square dancing lessons. It has helped immensely with my coordination.

I even bought one of those flouncey dresses to wear.

We dance by ourselves as I am not coordinated enough to dance with the others, but I am getting there.

The medical bills are just trickling in now. I go to see doctors about once a month and those are the leg, hearing and head doctors. I'm finished with the plastic surgeons, dentists and the urologists.

It took Shaneika two weeks to go over the existing medical bills and pay them. She discovered $32,000 of overcharging, but luckily for me, no one argues with Shaneika Mary Todd, descendant of some of the most prominent families in Lexington. In her veins runs the blood of slaves and masters, frontiersmen and washerwomen, statesmen and indentured servants, soldiers and runaways. Since she didn't take a percentage of the award money, I gave her a check for $25,000 and bought her a new baby goat.

I still can't get medical insurance.

After settling with Matt the expenses on the cottage and paying all my other outstanding bills, I still owed my daughter.

We fought over this.

She didn't want any money back, but I knew through Jake that she had had to take out loans to cover costs for me. I finally got her to agree to a four-year payment plan with interest. I wrote a check and deposited it into her account, which I had opened when she was a teenager. She still used it for private concerns.

Out of 1.5 million dollar first payment, most of it was gone after a few months of bill paying. I put $40,000 in my checking account and what was left put in CDs. I don't trust the stock market anymore. Thank goodness I had a good honey harvest this year. It's enough to see me through to the next payment from the city, which will be quite small in comparison to the first. I am still wondering if I should sell the Butterfly while she still looks good. I knew that I couldn't keep her up to her current standard.  Oh, well, like Scarlett O'Hara, I'll think about that tomorrow.

Things were looking up, so when the phone rang I didn't even bother to check the ID.  According to Jake's protocol, I was only supposed to answer numbers I knew.  Otherwise, the machine was to pick it up.

"Hello."

"Did you enjoy your beignet at Café du Monde?"  The caller laughed.  "What a gloomy pair you and your daughter make."

"Who's this?"

"I watched with binoculars from the shore.  A touching ceremony, dumping your husband's ashes out at sea."

"O'nan?"

"I'll be seeing you, Josiah."

Click.

# BONUS

## AN EXCITING CHAPTER FROM

# <u>DEATH BY BRIDLE</u>

# PROLOGUE

A door slammed.

Nine-year-old Lincoln Warfield Clark Todd was sleeping comfortably atop several bales of hay next to the stall of his mother's Thoroughbred stallion, Comanche, when the horse began pawing and snorting.

He thought little of it, as the black stallion was always restless and skittish. It wasn't until the horse began kicking his stall door that Linc sat up from his makeshift bed and rubbed his sleepy hazel eyes. "Whoa, boy. Nothing's gonna hurt ya while Linc's here," he murmured softly to the horse. "Go back to sleep."

It was then that he heard two loud voices coming from deep within the race-training complex. He looked at his cell phone. It was 2:30 in the morning. Linc crept over to soothe the horse by rubbing his velvety muzzle.

"Quiet, Comanche," Linc commanded the big Thoroughbred.

Both horse and boy strained to listen.

Comanche's ears lay flat against his gleaming black coat.

Linc held on to the horse's bridle as he wondered where the night watchman was. Probably watching TV in the owner's office.

A chair scraped across concrete. The voices became louder and more argumentative. A man called the other a "son of a bitch" and said, "you'll ruin me."

The young boy, heavy with excitement, crept forward among the hanging tack, leaning rakes, stacked bales of hay, and black plastic buckets stuffed with brushes, combs and hoof picks. Peeking around the corner he chewed on his lower lip, a habit his mother was trying to get him to quit.

At the far end of the stable corridor, two men stood facing each other like gunfighters.

He couldn't see them very well as only one yellow light glowed feebly from the ceiling.

Horses poked their shaggy heads out of their stalls, their walnut eyeballs wide and glassy with foreboding.

A washed-out-looking man drew his fists up, crying, "I'll kill you if you tell. I'll kill you. I swear I will."

A single light, dangling from a worn-out cord, swung slightly from a light breeze, creating eerie dancing shadows on the man's gray flesh. He fumbled toward the other man, who raised his arms in defense.

A spike of fear ran up Linc's back. He rose from his crouching position, gasping.

Both men swiveled, staring at him with dumbfounded irritation. One of the men thudded toward Linc.

The young boy ran in the opposite direction, but fell over a feed bucket, cracking his head on the concrete floor. His world went black.

It stayed black for a very long time.

# 1

Shaneika called at seven that morning, relating that Linc was in the hospital and asking me to come right away.

"I'll be there," I mumbled, wiping the sleep from my eyes. Pushing away Baby, my fawn English mastiff, I untangled myself from the bed sheets but Shaneika hung up before I could ask any questions.

I called my best friend Matt at his law office, informing him of the morning's call. Both he and Shaneika were my lawyers, often working together.

Matt asked that I keep him apprised of the situation. He replied that he had to go after I heard someone calling his name.

A woman. Hmmmm. I recognized that friendly sexy tone of voice and knew what it meant, but couldn't bother to think of that now.

Looking for Jake, I found him swimming laps in the heated infinity pool.

Jake had been my bodyguard/physician's assistant since my fall from a cliff when a rogue cop tried to kill me. That's a long story, one that I want to forget, but the cop is still on the loose.

My daughter assigned Jake to me. He really works for her.

Somewhere along the line, I crossed the no-no boundary and fell in love with Jake. But I have nothing to offer. I'm much older. My body is put together with glue and wire. I don't think it could survive a younger man's attention. What little money I have is tied up in paying medical bills and keeping my farm afloat. So when his contract is up this October, I'm going to send Jake away.

By the way, my name is Josiah Reynolds. My grandmother named me after a Hebrew king known for his righteousness.

I'm known for other things, not all of them nice.

Previously an art history professor, I now keep honeybees and sell honey at the Farmers' Market in Lexington, Kentucky. It's enough to get by on if I live on the cheap. I'll never get rich on honeybees. It's more a work of love.

I clutched my robe at the throat while leaning over the steaming water to get Jake's attention.

He rose up like Nix, the Norse god of lakes – water streaming from his long, blue-black hair and down his ruddy, muscular body. "What's up," he asked, wiping hair from his eyes. He looked at me from under thick, dark eyelashes.

The pool wasn't the only thing steaming.

"Shaneika called. Said her boy was in the hospital. Wants me to come. Can you drive?"

"Sure thing. Why's he in the hospital?"

"Don't know. Just told me he was and asked me to hurry."

"Okay, but you do your exercises first, have breakfast, take your medication and then we'll go."

I shook my head. "That will take too long. She wants me to come now."

Jake scowled. "I don't care what she wants. You're still on a medical schedule. You don't know how strenuous a day this will be. You'll need your therapy and medication to make sure you can endure today without a lot of pain."

The magic word – pain.

I was terrified of pain and would do most anything to avoid it. We never fight except about my pain medication. I want more – lots more of the pain medication – not the pain.

He was right and I knew it.

I dropped my robe and, in my jammies, got into the warm water. We did half an hour of stretching before Jake sent me to the showers while he made breakfast and got dressed himself.

Within minutes, we were racing toward the hospital.

CPSIA information can be obtained at www.ICGtesting.com
Printed in the USA
LVOW11s1631120814

398772LV00003B/241/P